"You're *asked.*

Wyatt answered nonchalantly. "Why not? You have horses to care for. You can't do that and watch two babies at the same time."

"I haven't forgotten you don't know anything about babies. Have you?"

He gave her a lazy smile, and Chloe's heart thumped with foolish anticipation.

"I haven't been around babies before," Wyatt agreed. "But I don't know anything about caring for horses, either. And from where I'm standing the babies seem to be the far safer of the two jobs."

Chloe couldn't help but laugh. "You may want to reevaluate that opinion after a couple of days."

Wyatt smiled. "How hard could the job be? Two babies and a little cooking. It'll be a vacation compared to the hours I usually put in."

Chloe managed to keep a straight face. "Good. I'm sure a vacation like this is just what you need."

Dear Reader,

The month of June makes me think of June brides, Father's Day and the first bloom of summer love. And Silhouette Romance is celebrating the start of summer with six wonderful books about love and romance.

Our BUNDLE OF JOY this month is delivered by Stella Bagwell's *The Tycoon's Tots*—her thirtieth Silhouette book. As her TWINS ON THE DOORSTEP miniseries continues, we finally discover who gets to keep those adorable babies...*and* find romance in the bargain.

Elizabeth August is back with her much-loved SMYTHESHIRE, MASSACHUSETTS series. In *The Determined Virgin* you'll meet a woman whose marriage of convenience is proving to be very *in*convenient, thanks to her intense attraction to her "in-name-only" husband.

BACHELOR GULCH is a little town that needs women, *and* the name of Sandra Steffen's brand-new miniseries. The fun begins in *Luke's Would-Be Bride* as a local bachelor falls for his feisty receptionist—the one woman in town *not* looking for a husband!

And there are plenty more compelling romances for you this month: A lovely lady rancher can't wait to hightail it out of Texas—till she meets her handsome new foreman in Leanna Wilson's *Lone Star Rancher*. A new husband can't bear to tell his amnesiac bride that the baby she's carrying isn't his, in *Her Forgotten Husband* by Anne Ha. And one lucky cowboy discovers a night of passion has just made him a daddy in Teresa Southwick's *The Bachelor's Baby*.

I hope you enjoy all of June's books!

Melissa Senate,
Senior Editor

Silhouette Romance

Please address questions and book requests to:
Silhouette Reader Service
U.S.: 3010 Walden Ave., P.O. Box 1325, Buffalo, NY 14269
Canadian: P.O. Box 609, Fort Erie, Ont. L2A 5X3

THE TYCOON'S TOTS

Stella Bagwell

Silhouette

ROMANCE™

Published by Silhouette Books

America's Publisher of Contemporary Romance

To Lloyd,
for all those inspiring speeches
you used to give me.
Love always.

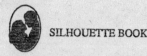 SILHOUETTE BOOKS

ISBN 0-373-19228-2

THE TYCOON'S TOTS

Copyright © 1997 by Stella Bagwell

This edition published by arrangement with Harlequin Books S.A.

® and TM are trademarks of Harlequin Books S.A., used under license. Trademarks indicated with ® are registered in the United States Patent and Trademark Office, the Canadian Trade Marks Office and in other countries.

Printed in U.S.A.

Bundles
of JOY

Dear Reader,

It's always a special treat for me to have the opportunity to speak to you directly and say a big thank-you for buying and reading my books—all thirty of them—down through the years!

Writing romances isn't an easy job, but it *is* a very fulfilling one. I like to think I'm spreading a little love to each and every one of you through my books.

I'm especially proud of *The Tycoon's Tots*, which features not one, but two adorable babies and two people who desperately want to be their parents. It also happens to be a continuation of my TWINS ON THE DOORSTEP miniseries.

The Tycoon's Tots, as with the other two books of the series, is all about family and what it means to a woman to be a part of a family, yet also have one of her very own. After all, we women don't just stop at being a lover, or wife. More often than not we're also a mother, a daughter, or a sister, and our love doesn't just encompass a man, it reaches over the entire family and makes each relationship within it a very special thing. I think you'll see such is the case with my heroines, the Murdock sisters.

It was a delight for me to write TWINS ON THE DOORSTEP and tell you how two babies not only create chaos and change in the Murdock family, but also bring lasting love to Justine, Rose and Chloe. I hope each of their stories will touch a spot in your heart as they did mine and that you'll enjoy reading them as much as I enjoyed writing them.

Love and God Bless,

Books by Stella Bagwell

STELLA BAGWELL

sold her first book to Silhouette in November 1985. Now thirty novels later she is still thrilled to see her books in print and can't imagine having any other job than that of writing about two people falling in love.

She lives in a small town in southeastern Oklahoma with her husband of twenty-six years. She has one son and daughter-in-law.

Prologue

Wyatt Sanders picked up the plain white envelope lying atop the leather duffel bag and pulled out a one-page letter. He'd read the words so many times now, he practically knew them by heart, but he still felt compelled to read it again one last time before he left Houston.

Dear Wyatt,

I know it's been awhile since we last talked, so hearing from me now, like this, must be a shock for you. Believe me, I never wanted to be a burden to you. Especially after Daddy died. You have your own life to live. But there seems to be no one else I can turn to for help.

It's a long story, but I've gotten myself into a mess. I didn't want you to know how things were with me— at least not until I had the chance to fix them. Just please don't reproach me for making bad choices. I never was as strong as you, Wyatt.

As of now I'm in a mental health facility in Las Cruces, New Mexico. But I'm going to get better.

Promise. Until then, I want you to go get my babies and take them home with you. They told me their father is dead now. I'm not sure I believe them, but if he is, I know you'll be a good father to my twins, Wyatt. They need you now and so do I.

Below his sister's signature was the name of a family and a ranch in Hondo, New Mexico, where the babies were supposedly staying. Wyatt had never heard his sister mention the family or the place before. But he would find them. It was the only way he could help his sister now.

Chapter One

Chloe Murdock galloped the chestnut around the track a second time, then slowed him to a trot. He wasn't ready to quit their run, and Chloe had to strain against the reins to remind him who was boss.

She'd just gotten the horse in check when she noticed the man standing at the top of the hill, a few yards away from the stable. He was looking in her direction, his hand shading his eyes, even though he was wearing a pair of dark glasses.

It wasn't unusual for a man to visit the ranch. Men often stopped by to inquire about buying a horse or bull. The Bar M had always been known for its good stock and that hadn't changed even though her father, Tomas, had died and no longer ran the place.

Yet even from this distance, Chloe got the impression that this man in his khaki slacks and expensive leather jacket was not here to buy or sell stock. At least not the four-legged kind she was familiar with.

By the time she reached the top of the hill, the chestnut was still dancing with the urge to run. His sides were heaving and his flared nostrils blew streams of vapor into the crisp morning air. The man on the ground kept a careful distance from the woman and the fired up thoroughbred.

"Hello," she said to him. "I'm Chloe Murdock. Can I help you?"

Not certain he could trust her or the horse, Wyatt remained several steps away.

"I'm Wyatt Sanders. The woman up at the house told me I would find you down here." Innate good manners had him pulling off his sunglasses and slipping them inside his shirt pocket.

Chloe was a woman who'd never been that impressed with men, good-looking or otherwise, but she had to admit this one was quite striking. His hair was as black and shiny as a crow's wing and slicked straight back from a wide forehead. His hooded gray eyes were a cool and startling contrast against his darkly tanned skin. Though his lips were compressed in a thin line at the moment, she got the impression of chiseled fullness. There was money and city polish written from the toes of his brown Italian loafers to the top of his expensive haircut.

"If you're looking for a racehorse, I'm not inclined to sell. A few months ago, I did let a five-year-old go in a claiming race, but the ten I have now are all young and," she flashed him a charming smile, "fast."

Wyatt hadn't been ready for the sight of this woman, nor the sexy tilt of her berry colored lips. He'd been expecting a cowgirl of course—what else would one find on a ranch?—but all the cowgirls he'd ever seen in Houston wore skin-tight blue jeans, overdone makeup and big hairdos.

But this girl, or more rightly this slip of a woman, sitting astride the nervous thoroughbred was nothing like that. She was wearing jeans all right, but they were black and loose fitting with the hems tucked into a pair of brown western boots that had intricate stitching on the tall tops.

An old gray rugby shirt served as her blouse. In spite of the cool air, the neck was unbuttoned and the sleeves were pushed up to her elbows to show a pair of slender but strongly muscled forearms. Her straight hair was the color of rich burgundy wine. While the crown was covered with a red baseball cap, the cape of it lying against her back shone like red silk in the morning sun.

There was no makeup or artificial color to be found on her face, yet she looked anything but pale. The wind had blushed her cheeks and lips and her deep green eyes glittered like twin emeralds as she looked down at him from her lofty perch on the horse's back.

"Actually," he said, "I'm...not looking to buy a race-horse."

Her winged brows arched at him. "Oh. Then you're here about a bull. Well, you'll have to see my sister, Rose."

"I'm not here about a bull, either. I'm here..." He paused as he realized all the things he'd planned on saying, all the questions his mind had dwelled on these past weeks, were fast slipping away as he looked up at Chloe Murdock's face. She was nothing like the woman he'd thought he'd be dealing with, and the difference had thrown him.

"Yes?" she prompted.

"I'm here to talk to you."

The chestnut was hot and if Chloe didn't keep him moving while he cooled down, his muscles would be stiff tomorrow. She had no intention of letting that happen, no matter what business this man wanted to discuss.

"You'll have to let me put Banjo on the walker."

She reined the horse away from him and headed over to the stable. Wyatt followed, carefully stepping around piles of horse manure as he went.

At the stable, Chloe jerked off the small racing saddle, tossed it over the fence, then led the tall chestnut over to

where three other horses were being mechanically led
around a large circle.

After she'd fastened Banjo's lead rope to one of the free
arms and put the horses in motion again, she walked over
to the stranger and extended her hand to him.

"Sorry about the interruption, er—Mr. Sanders, is it?"

Wyatt hadn't planned on shaking Chloe Murdock's
hand, but he found it impossible to rebuff her. The genuine
warmth he sensed about her compelled him to remain a
gentleman.

"Yes," he answered. "It's Sanders. Wyatt Sanders."

She had a healthy grip for someone with such a small
hand. He could feel calluses on her palms, something he'd
never encountered on a woman before. But then he'd never
known any woman who actually did manual labor such as
this one obviously did.

"Well, Mr. Sanders, what can I help you with today?
Are you looking for land in this area?"

Her assumption put a quirk of amusement on his lips.
"What makes you think that?" he found himself asking.

Chloe shrugged as she once again eyed him with open
curiosity. "You're obviously not from around here. I
thought you might be in real estate."

The wind was playing with her shoulder length hair,
whipping a few strands across her face. She had pale
golden skin, he noticed, with one freckle a fraction above
the edge of her upper lip.

He forced himself to drop her hand, but his eyes refused
to leave her face. Incredibly, she was the sexiest woman
he'd ever seen. "I'm an oilman from Houston, Texas," he
told her.

She smiled at that and Wyatt felt something inside him
jerk as though he'd been stung by an arrow.

"A Texas oilman," she repeated with faint amusement.
"What are you doing out here in New Mexico? Looking
to buy or lease the mineral rights in this area? I wasn't

aware this part of the state had petroleum resources. 'Course, I know there's the big Conoco field over by Eunice and there's oil down at Lordsburg, but you're talking at least a couple of hundred miles from here. And that's all desert land. You're in the mountains now.''

So. Wyatt had noticed. One minute he'd been in the desert, then before he'd realized it the terrain had changed, and he'd been winding through forested mountains and lush green valley floor. The change in landscape had surprised him almost as much as the sight of Chloe Murdock. "I'm not here looking for oil. It's something more personal.''

Her eyes narrowed at his evasiveness. "Personal? Dear God, I hope you're not going to tell me it has something to do with my father Tomas,'' she said without preamble.

"It does. In a way,'' he said and was struck by how much he wanted to avoid the issue that had brought him to this ranch and this woman. It would have been pleasant to simply talk to her a few more minutes.

"Look, Mr. Sanders, my father has been dead for several months. I'm not trying to make excuses, but whatever he owes you, we didn't know about it. We've been trying to pay off his debts, but for right now, all I can say is you'll just have to stand in line and wait your turn.''

The memory of Belinda's coffin being lowered into the ground suddenly flashed through Wyatt's mind. "What your father owes me could never be repaid.''

"I beg your pardon?''

His gray eyes clashed with the spark of her green ones. "You heard what I said. Your father took something from me that can't be compensated.''

Chloe was fast losing her patience with this man. He'd obviously come here for money. Why didn't he just spit it out and be done with all this dallying around?

"I've always heard Texans go at things at a slower pace, but do you think for this one time you could speed things along and get to the point? I have lots of work waiting on me and the morning is already half gone.''

His jaw clenched. ''Your father can't give my sister back to me,'' he said tightly.

Chloe drew in a sharp little breath. ''Who are you?''

He took a step closer. ''I told you who I was.''

Her full lips twisted at his response. ''An oilman from Houston. So what connection do you have with me or this ranch?''

Her voice, which up until a moment ago had been warm and lilting, was now sharp-edged and demanding. ''My sister was Belinda Waller and your father killed her,'' he said flatly.

The first spill Chloe had taken on the galloping track had knocked the wind from her lungs and scrambled her senses. For several minutes she'd been unable to tell if the ground was really the sky or visa versa. Hearing Belinda Waller had a brother left her feeling as though she'd just taken another walloping fall.

''My father didn't kill anybody,'' she finally managed to say. ''Now if you'll excuse me, I've got work to do.''

Turning, she left him standing on the muddy hillside. She knew he would follow her. He hadn't come all this way to let things go at that. But Chloe was too shaken, too stunned to simply stand stock-still while the man bored holes in her with those cold gray eyes.

''I'm not going to be put off, Ms. Murdock. We have things to talk about.''

She glanced over her shoulder to see he'd joined her in the long, dim stable. For a moment all Chloe could think was that he looked like an alien standing there on the wood shavings in his crisply ironed cotton and softly worn leather. He wasn't from this world, so why had he come here?

With a flip of her wrist, she jerked the baseball cap from

her head and shook her hair back from her face. "Then talk. Who's stopping you?"

His teeth ground together as he watched her slap the cap back on her head, then toss a shovel into a wheelbarrow and push it into an empty stall.

"I'd think you'd have the courtesy to go up to the house and give me your undivided attention."

Chloe didn't bother to look at him. Instead, she scooped up a shovelful of dirty wood shavings and horse manure. "I don't have time to go through social niceties with you. And even if I did, I wouldn't."

Oilmen, even the ones like himself who worked in plush offices and drove Mercedeses, were used to blunt, rough talk interspersed with a wide range of four-letter words. It went with the business. But that was from his male counterparts. The women he encountered were always full of sugar and ready to give him all the attention he wanted. He couldn't believe Chloe Murdock was dismissing him as though he were no better than the stuff she was tossing into the wheelbarrow.

"I didn't come here to fight with you," he said, trying his best to hold onto his temper.

"After what your sister did to my family, I can't believe you had the gall to come here at all."

Wyatt didn't know what had come over him. Any other time, he would have taken hold of her shoulder and physically made her turn and face him. Instead, he found himself staring, fascinated by her rounded behind as she bent over the shovel, the fluid movements of her body as she pitched another scoopful.

"Flinging accusations at each other isn't going to get us anywhere," he said.

"I can't say I *want* to get anywhere with you," she said with a strained grunt as she forced the shovel point down through the packed shavings.

"You're not making this any easier for either of us."

Anger surged through Chloe, but she tried to take it out on the shovel instead of him. "Believe me, Mr. Sanders, nothing has been easy since my father died. And as for anyone killing anybody, I'd say your sister was the major contributor to the heart attack that killed Tomas. She was blackmailing him, you know. Milking him of his money, and his self-respect. What kind of woman would do that?"

"I think—"

Before he could say more, Chloe flung the shovel to the ground and whirled on him. Her eyes were shooting sparks as hot as her auburn hair. "Tell me, Mr. Sanders, what sort of woman would leave two little helpless babies on a porch and never look back? She didn't care if they lived or died, so don't come here whining about the loss of your sister. You'll not get sympathy from me or anyone else on this ranch!"

Since he'd learned of Belinda's death, Wyatt had been full of outrage and pain. He hadn't stopped to think the Murdock family might be feeling as injured as he.

"I'm not looking for sympathy. Especially from you. I'll be the first to admit that Belinda had her problems. I didn't know about the twins or anything. Not until—" he paused and drew in a heavy breath "—it was already too late. But whatever her faults, she didn't deserve to die in a mental hospital for criminals!"

Chloe could see real grief on Wyatt Sanders's face and it touched her in spite of who he was and all that Belinda had done to her family. "I didn't want your sister to die. None of my family wanted any such thing to happen."

"Maybe not. But your father was the reason she was in trouble with the law in the first place."

Chloe's jaw dropped. The man was obviously as crazy as his sister had been. "How could you possibly think such a thing? Your sister was a dangerous, unstable woman. I'm sorry if that pains you, but that's the way it was."

Tight-lipped, he said, "My sister would never have been

prompted to do the things she did if your father hadn't seduced her and ruined her life.''

Chloe had always been cursed with a quick temper. Growing up, she'd often been punished for her angry outbursts. Ladies don't fight, her mother had gently scolded Chloe when she'd come home one afternoon from grammar school with a fat lip. It hadn't made any difference to Lola when Chloe'd tried to explain she'd punched the playground bully in the face because he'd been calling her best friend ugly names.

According to Lola, little girls didn't lose their tempers and they certainly didn't resort to physical violence. It was a lesson from her mother that Chloe always remembered, but had never fully learned. She was too much like her father, she supposed. She couldn't sit idly on her hands when an innocent person was being wronged.

Stepping from the stall, Chloe walked to within a step of Wyatt Sanders and looked him square in the eye. ''I don't know who did the seducing, my father or your sister. And I hardly imagine that you could know, either. But I do know your sister had no business becoming involved with a married man twice her age.''

There was some truth to what Chloe Murdock was saying, but Wyatt knew there were always two sides to every story. And he couldn't believe Belinda had decided to walk down the wrong path all by herself.

''And your father had no business getting a woman half his age pregnant!''

''You're damn right he didn't,'' Chloe hotly agreed. ''My mother was an invalid at the time he was sleeping around with your sister! His behavior was lower than a snake's belly, but that doesn't change things. We could stand here all day flinging accusations at each other, but it wouldn't bring my father or your sister back.''

A part of Wyatt admired this woman for her nononsense bluntness. He couldn't stand people who philosophized a point to death and in the end wound up saying nothing. But in the matter of his sister, Wyatt couldn't simply put it all behind him and say what's done is done. Even though they hadn't been particularly close, he'd loved Belinda. And he couldn't help but feel guilty because he hadn't been there for her when she'd needed him the most.

He let out a long, heavy breath. "Actually, I didn't come here to fling accusations. I would like to know exactly what happened between my sister and Mr. Murdock, but that can wait. My main concern now is my little niece and nephew."

Chloe felt as if ice water had suddenly been dashed in her face. Adam and Anna, the twin babies that this man's sister had left on the Bar M doorstep, were her half sister and brother. Chloe considered them her babies now and she'd already had a lawyer working on adoption proceedings. If Wyatt Sanders had any notion of trying to take them away from her, he might as well forget it here and now.

"There's no need for you to be concerned. Adam and Anna are in perfect health and growing."

"I understand you've had them here on the ranch ever since—"

Chloe couldn't prevent a sneer from twisting her lips. "Your sister dumped them, you mean? Yes, the county judge granted me and my sisters temporary custody. Then later, when we learned they were really our half brother and sister we knew they actually belonged here anyway."

His eyes remained on her face and Chloe got the impression he was trying to gauge her or size her up in some way. She didn't like the feeling at all.

"Then you think the twins belong here?"

"Of course. They're Murdocks. This is the Murdock home."

"You know for certain that your father sired them? Were DNA tests performed?"

Under different circumstances Chloe would have howled with laughter, but she could hardly find her sense of humor with Wyatt Sanders standing a few inches away looking as though he were ready to pounce at any given moment.

"Believe me, Mr. Sanders, there's no need for tests to be done. For legal purposes I suppose we could have a test run to see if we truly are siblings. But once you see the twins, you'll know that would be a waste of time and money." She folded her arms across her breasts. "Besides, I'm going to adopt the babies. Maybe you should understand that right now."

Chloe Murdock's announcement stunned him. He'd been told by New Mexican authorities that Belinda's children were under the care of the Murdock family, which consisted of three sisters. Chloe, the youngest, had direct charge over the twins. But none of the child welfare people had mentioned anything about her plans to adopt the children.

What did it all mean? Wyatt wondered. Was he going to have a fight on his hands?

"I had no idea you intended to adopt the babies," he finally said.

"I'm not surprised. We weren't even aware Belinda had a brother. As far as I know your sister never mentioned you. Not even when we talked to her in jail."

Wyatt didn't know if it was Chloe Murdock or what she was saying that was having such a strong effect on him. But suddenly his insides were shaking as if he'd just woken from a two-day drunk.

"You saw my sister while she was jailed?"

Chloe nodded. It wasn't one of her more pleasant memories. But she and her sisters, Justine and Rose, had felt compelled to talk to the woman. She'd known things about their father that only she could tell them. And Belinda had told them some things in her own disturbed, fragmented way. Chloe had come away from the county jail feeling both saddened and sickened. From what she'd seen, Belinda Waller had once been a beautiful young woman, but drugs and alcohol had ruined her looks, her mind, and subsequently her very life. It was such a waste.

"How was she then? How long was that before she died?"

Chloe shrugged. "Two or three weeks probably. As far as how she was, I can't really say. I didn't know her beforehand."

Wyatt felt weak and sick. And he wondered why he'd ever left Houston to come here. But of course, deep down he knew it was simply for the babies. He felt he owed Belinda that much.

Turning away from Chloe, Wyatt walked to the end of the long stable and stared out the open doorway at the mountain range rising directly behind the ranch.

It didn't seem possible that his family was gone now. His mother had simply left. His father had been killed. And now Belinda was dead. The only close relatives Wyatt had left were the twins.

"Mr. Sanders? Are you all right?"

He turned slowly to see Chloe standing just behind him. She looked genuinely concerned for him, which was quite a switch from a few moments ago when he'd gotten the impression she wanted to wham the side of his head with her shovel.

"I was just thinking about Belinda," he said, then with a sigh he swiped a hand through his coal black hair. "She was beautiful and outgoing. One of those bubbly kind of people who laughed a lot. She loved excitement and always liked to stay on the go." His expression grim, he glanced away from her. "But her traveling days are all over now."

Whatever Chloe felt about Belinda Waller, she harbored no malice toward this man. As far as she and her family knew, he had nothing to do with the damage his sister had done to their father and their ranch. It would serve no purpose to describe to him the pathetic creature she'd seen locked behind bars. He obviously didn't know what his sister had become. And Chloe hardly wanted to be the one to tell him.

"Well, we might as well go up to the house so you can see the twins," she said, while telling herself the sooner he saw the babies, the sooner he would leave the ranch. "Aunt Kitty is probably feeding them a snack about now."

"Earlier, at the house, a small woman with gray hair answered the door. Was that your aunt?"

Chloe nodded and Wyatt said, "I figured she was the housekeeper or nanny or something."

"We're all family around here," she told him, her voice laced with pride.

"I see," he said. "And she helps take care of the twins while you're doing this?" He gestured around the large stable.

The way he said *this* made it sound as if she were no better than a common ditch digger. And she suddenly decided it was a shame the inside of this man wasn't as nice as the outside. But then, in her experience, men were usually lacking beneath the surface.

"She does," Chloe answered his question. "Aunt Kitty loves the twins as much as me and my sisters."

He didn't say anything to that and Chloe wondered what he was thinking and why he was really here. She somehow knew she hadn't heard everything from him yet.

"Well, right now I have to get the horses off the walker. If you'd rather not wait, you can go on up to the house without me," she told him.

Wyatt figured if he was smart, he wouldn't wait. He'd go see the babies without this woman's interference. But he didn't always do the smart thing. Believing Belinda's happy stories proved that much.

"I'll wait. Is there anything I can help you with?"

Surprised by his offer, she looked at him. Not as a threat, but simply as a man. "I wouldn't want you to dirty yourself."

There wasn't anything he needed to prove to this woman. Her opinion of him didn't matter at all. Yet the idea that she thought of him as soft, pricked his ego as nothing had in years. "I've been known to get a little dirt under my fingernails before."

She gave him a dry little smile. "Scratching and clawing your way to the top, I suppose?"

"You find something wrong with ambition, Ms. Murdock?"

"Not when it's aimed in the right direction, Mr. Sanders."

Brushing past him, she walked out of the stable to leave Wyatt standing by the empty stall. For a moment he considered following her, but then he decided there wouldn't be much point in it. This was her turf, and she obviously figured he'd be more of a hindrance than a help.

It took her only a matter of a few minutes to return the four horses to their stalls. Wyatt stood silently by, watching her work and wondering if this was how she spent all of her time here on this isolated New Mexican ranch. In his opinion it was a shame to see a beautiful woman like her buried in such a place.

Once she was ready to go, Wyatt followed her out of the stable and along the beaten path leading back to the house. Along the way they passed several barns and a maze of connecting metal pens.

Wyatt didn't see any cattle except one bull lying near a mound of alfalfa hay. Closer to the house, in a small wooden corral, a black calf poked its head through the fence and bawled loudly.

"You'll get your bottle soon enough, Martin," Chloe told the calf. "You're not the only one around here who's hungry."

"Where's his mother? Can't she feed him?" Wyatt asked as they walked on at a brisk clip. Did the woman move at this pace all day, he wondered. If she did, she had to feel like hell by nightfall. And weren't there any cowboys around to help?

"His mother is dead. My sister Rose and I take turns hand-feeding him." Chloe didn't go on to tell him that Martin's mother was killed when Belinda torched a section of the ranch. It was a horrible scene she hated to think about, much less relate to him.

A few moments later, the two of them entered a small courtyard landscaped with an assortment of desert plants, a couple of piñon pines and redwood lawn furniture.

A ground-level porch made a square with the back of the house. Wyatt followed her across one end of it, through a screen door and into a warm, cluttered kitchen. Two steps inside the room, Wyatt stopped dead in his tracks as he spotted two red-headed babies sitting side by side in a pair of high chairs.

These were his sister's children, the only close relatives he had left. Yet incredibly they looked like the woman standing next to him.

"Aunt Kitty, this is Wyatt Sanders."

Wyatt tore his gaze away from the babies to see the petite gray-haired woman had joined them. She was wiping her hands on a tea towel and looking Wyatt over with open suspicion.

"Yes, he told me his name when he came to the door. I see you found Chloe," she told him.

He nodded politely toward the older woman, but before he could get a word out, Chloe said, "Did he tell you he's Belinda Waller's brother?"

Kitty's face grew ashen and her wide gaze flew from

her niece to the dark-haired stranger. "Belinda's brother?" she asked in a hoarse whisper. "We didn't know she had a brother! What are you doing here?"

Wyatt turned to Chloe and wondered, not for the first time, what his next words were going to do to her.

"I'm here to take the twins home. With me," he said quietly.

Chapter Two

Now was not the time for Chloe to panic or lose her temper. She had to show this man he didn't scare her. The twins were hers! He couldn't simply walk in and take them away from her!

Her gaze didn't waver as she met his cool gray eyes. "The twins *are* home, Mr. Sanders. Like I said earlier, they're Murdocks, and the Bar M has been our home for more than thirty years."

She'd already told him her intention of adopting the twins, so it hardly surprised Wyatt to hear her calling this ranch their rightful home. But he had other ideas. The quicker Ms. Chloe Murdock realized that the better off they'd all be.

"I think you're forgetting the babies are half Sanders."

Like a mammy dog guarding her litter, Chloe stood her ground. "Excuse me, but your sister's name was Waller, not Sanders."

He grimaced as though Chloe's point had little conse-quence on the matter. "She was married and divorced several years ago. But by any name, her babies are my niece and nephew.''

"And they're my half brother and sister. I think even you can admit that.''

Groaning, Kitty reached for a nearby chair and wilted into it.

Wyatt turned his gaze back to the twins who were busily concentrating on eating graham crackers. Soggy crumbs dotted their bibs and cheeks and clung to their fingers in gooey clumps. They seemed perfectly contented and their sweet, intelligent faces went straight to Wyatt's heart.

"How old are they?'' he asked.

"Ten months,'' she answered, then volunteered. "They can crawl and pull up now.''

Fascinated by the sight of them, Wyatt walked over and hunkered down to their level. The babies weren't exactly identical, but close to it. They both had green eyes, chubby round faces and dimpled cheeks. The girl's hair was a bright red cap of curls while the boy's was the very same dark auburn as Chloe Murdock's.

Even to him, it was plain to see they were her brother and sister. Wyatt couldn't deny that. Yet they were a part of him, too. He couldn't forget or dismiss that fact.

"Hello, you two,'' he said, suddenly feeling awkward and foolishly emotional. "I'm your Uncle Wyatt.''

The sound of his voice caught the twins' attention and both children stopped their chewing to give him a closer look.

"We named them Adam and Anna,'' Chloe said as she came up behind the three of them.

He looked over his shoulder at her. "That isn't what my sister named them?''

"No. For a long time we had no idea who they belonged to or what their names were. So we named them our-selves.''

One dark brow arched at her. "Don't you think you were being rather presumptuous?"

Fury washed through Chloe but she tried her best to squash it down. "And don't you think these two little darlings deserved something better than Baby Boy or Baby Girl? Don't you think they deserved better than to be left in a laundry basket on a porch? There was no one around when your sister dumped them and to this day we still don't know how long they had been there before my sister Justine found them. Apparently Belinda had no idea that a coyote or anything could have dragged them off and killed them. Or maybe she did," Chloe couldn't help adding.

Wyatt straightened to his full height and looked at her through narrow gray eyes. "Whatever my sister was, she wasn't a murderer."

"I don't think you really know what your sister was," she said flatly. "But that's beside the point now. The babies are mine. You'll not take them from this ranch."

"Chloe, perhaps—" Kitty began only to have her niece wave a quieting hand at her.

"What makes you think you have a right to them?" Wyatt asked coolly.

"What makes you think you do?" she countered.

Wyatt glanced down at the babies, then turned his attention to the room they were in. It wasn't anything like the spotless kitchen in his Houston condominium. There were pots and pans hanging on one wall, plants lining every available windowsill, and dirty dishes stacked on the table and cabinet counter. Something resembling pinto beans had boiled over on the cook-stove and dripped down over the control knobs. In one corner an ironing board was piled with clothes. Whether they were clean or not, Wyatt couldn't tell.

"I think the twins deserve a better life than this," he said bluntly.

Ladies didn't resort to physical violence be damned, Chloe thought, as she stepped up and jabbed her finger hard in the middle of Wyatt Sanders's chest.

"And I think you wouldn't know a better life if it reached up and bit you in the butt!"

Momentarily stunned by her unexpected response, Wyatt could only stare at her. She wasn't only sexy, she was the wildest little thing he'd ever come across.

"And if you think this place is so bad," she went on, "I suggest you leave. Now! Before I call the sheriff."

Kitty gasped. "Chloe! There's no need to call Roy. Mr. Sanders is—"

"Who's Roy?" Wyatt asked, seemingly unruffled by her threat.

"The sheriff."

"My brother-in-law."

The two women spoke at once, but Wyatt managed to decipher the message. It irked him that she wanted to drag the law into this, even if the sheriff was her family. But it didn't surprise him. Chloe Murdock didn't appear to be a woman who'd give up or give in without a fight.

Before he could say anything, Anna began to whine and fuss. Wyatt instinctively turned toward the baby, but Chloe instantly leapt between them.

"Don't you dare touch her!" she hissed at him, then lifted the little girl into her arms.

With a glare as cold as gray granite, Wyatt pulled a pen and small business card from a pocket inside his jacket, then quickly wrote something across the back.

"This is where I'll be staying," he said flatly. "When you decide to calm down, maybe we can talk about this sensibly."

Calm down? She wanted to leave her handprint along the side of his face!

"I really doubt I'll ever get the urge to talk to you, Mr.

Sanders, so you might as well go back to Houston and play oilman.''

''We'll see, Ms. Murdock,'' he said, then turned and walked out the same door she'd brought him through earlier.

Once he was truly out of sight, Chloe glanced at her stricken aunt, then still holding Anna, raced out of the kitchen.

''Chloe!''

Kitty jumped from her chair and grabbing Adam hurried after her niece. She found her in the living room peering out the long paned windows which overlooked the front yard.

''What are you doing?''

Clutching Anna even tighter, Chloe watched the expensive dark blue car pull away from the house and head down the drive. ''Making sure that—man is gone!''

''He'll be back, Chloe,'' Kitty said grimly. ''You might as well get ready for it. Didn't you notice how cool he was? I got the impression he's here for the long haul.''

Chloe turned away from the windows, and for the first time since Wyatt Sanders had announced his intentions, she allowed the fear she was feeling to show on her face. ''Dear God, what are we going to do, Aunt Kitty? There isn't any way Wyatt Sanders can take the babies, is there?''

In a weary daze, Kitty sank onto the couch and wiped a hand across her forehead. ''I have no idea, Chloe. Custody rights are very unpredictable nowadays.''

Chloe looked down at Anna's sweet face. She couldn't imagine her life without the babies. She refused to even try.

''Maybe you should call the lawyer who's handling your adoption proceedings.''

Chloe set Anna on the tiled floor and the little girl immediately crawled over to the couch and pulled up beside her aunt's knee.

"I'll call him right now." She snatched up the phone book, quickly searched for the number, then punched it through. After a few brief words with a secretary, she hung up. "He's out of town and won't be back for another week or more."

"Just our luck. Maybe you could discuss it with his associate."

"If I have to, I will. But right now, I'm going to finish the chores at the stable, then drive over to Justine's. She and Rose need to know someone is trying to take our brother and sister!"

Two hours later and several miles north on the Pardee ranch, Chloe paced around her sister's living room.

"Chloe, you're going to have to calm down," Justine insisted from her seat on the couch. "It's not like the man tried to physically carry the twins out of the house."

Chloe looked over at her very pregnant sister. It probably wasn't good to dump this sort of stress on her. Even though the baby wasn't due for another eight or ten weeks, Justine had already been suffering false labor pains.

"I guess I shouldn't have come over here bothering you with this," Chloe mumbled regretfully. "But I didn't know what else to do."

Justine waved away her words. "Chloe, honey, Adam and Anna are my brother and sister, too. I was going to have to know about Wyatt sooner or later. I just find it incredible that Belinda Waller had a brother. Why hadn't we heard from him before now?"

Chloe threw up her arms in a gesture of helplessness. "I got the impression he didn't know much about Belinda, or what she'd been up to lately. At least, not the way we knew her," Chloe added with a shudder. Neither she, Justine, nor their older sister Rose, who'd very nearly been injured by Belinda's arson, would ever forget the woman.

"Do you think he's on the up-and-up? Maybe he's no better than Belinda," Justine mused aloud. "If that's the case, there's no court in the country that would consider giving him custody of the twins."

With a weary shake of her head, Chloe sat down beside her sister on the couch. "Wyatt Sanders doesn't appear to be anything like Belinda. He says he's an oilman. And I tell you, Justine, the man has money. If he doesn't, he's doing a good job of faking it."

Justine glanced at her wristwatch. "Roy is testifying in court now. But he should be through by late this evening. I'll call and let him know what's going on. He'll run a check on Mr. Wyatt Sanders and then we'll have a better idea what to do."

Chloe gave her a crooked grin. "You know, it's rather nice having the sheriff of Lincoln County in the family."

Justine chuckled and patted her protruding belly. "I definitely think so."

There was no doubt that Justine was happy now. She and Roy Pardee had married back in July a few weeks after the twins first showed up on the ranch's front porch. They loved each other passionately. So much so that Chloe sometimes looked at the two of them with awe and envy.

At twenty-four, Chloe was only two years younger than Justine, and four younger than Rose. But she felt she was a lifetime away from having a family of her own—the sort of family that both her sisters had now.

"Maybe you should go to him," Justine suggested after a stretch of silence. "Tell the man how it is with you and why you want the babies so badly."

The look Chloe shot Justine said she must be losing her mind. "Never! There's no way I'd tell that arrogant bast..." She caught herself before the whole word burst from her mouth. "That arrogant man such an intimate detail about myself. Besides, I really doubt he could or would sympathize with my sterile condition. Especially when he looks like he could produce all the babies he wanted!''

Sighing, Justine reached for the cup of decaffeinated coffee sitting on the end table by her elbow. ''Chloe, you're much too sensitive about your condition. It's nothing to be ashamed of. It wasn't your fault you had an infection and it left you too scarred to have children.''

Chloe frowned at her sister. ''Sure. That's easy for you to say. You're about to give your husband his second child. I can't give a man anything.''

Justine rolled her eyes. ''That's ridiculous of you to think such a thing!''

Dropping her head, Chloe looked away from her sister. ''Ridiculous or not, I don't want any man, friend or foe, to know that I'm sterile. You know what happened the last time I tried to be honest and open with a man!''

Her expression full of concern, Justine said, ''Richard was a selfish fool. I'm sure he's realized a thousand times what he lost when he broke your engagement.''

Chloe groaned. ''Justine, that was four years ago. You don't see the man knocking down my door to beg me to come back to him, do you?''

Frowning, Justine waved away her words. ''I, for one, thank God, he hasn't. He wasn't nearly good enough for you.''

Chloe looked at her sister. ''Well, you don't have to worry about Richard or any man walking me down the aisle. No man wants a woman who is barren.''

Justine shook her head. ''You're wrong, Chloe. Children are a wonderful addition, but they don't make a marriage.''

Maybe her sister truly believed that, but Chloe knew better. She'd been rejected by a man she'd hoped to marry, culled like a cow that couldn't calf. She never wanted to go through that sort of pain and humiliation again.

As for Wyatt Sanders, she would never tell the man she couldn't have children. She'd fight for the twins any way she could, but not that way.

Chapter Three

"Wyatt, sugar, I can understand how cute and sweet your sister's babies are, but I don't believe you've stopped to consider what sort of care and responsibility it would take to raise them to adulthood. Not to mention the expense."

Wyatt gazed out the Ruidoso motel room window as Sandra's voice droned in his ear. It had been several hours since his encounter with Ms. Chloe Murdock, and he was still smarting from her high-handed attitude. He'd called Sandra back in Houston, thinking she would understand and commiserate with him. But so far she wasn't making him feel a bit better.

He'd met her through a mutual friend and had found her blond, blue-eyed looks and classic taste in clothes reminiscent of a young Grace Kelly. He'd dated her a few times and the idea of proposing marriage to her had once crossed his mind. Not because he'd been in love with her. He hadn't been. In fact, Wyatt was sure he'd never felt the real thing. He wasn't even sure it existed. But he and Sandra had got on well enough and, though she liked money, she never put any emotional demands on him. Since he'd turned thirty the idea of marrying was starting to appeal to him, and he'd thought they might make a compatible team.

But he'd quickly learned Sandra wasn't wife material for him or any man. Her career consumed the bigger part of her time, and since Wyatt had started talking about bringing the twins home to live with him, he could see that motherhood was not her forte either. Thank goodness, he and Sandra were no more than good friends now.

"I know babies require a lot of care, Sandra. But I have the money to provide them with a good nanny, and later on a college education. I can give them most anything they'll need to have a relatively good life. And I think I owe them that much."

"I can't see that you *owe* them anything, Wyatt. Sure, they're your sister's kids, but that doesn't mean you have to sacrifice your life for them."

His brows drew together at her insensitive comment. The idea that all women were born with maternal instincts was a bunch of malarkey. Sandra had just proven it. And then there was his mother, whom he hadn't heard a word from in the past twenty-six years. Dear Lord, had Belinda been just as uncaring of her twins? No, he didn't believe it for a minute.

"I'd hardly call it a sacrifice, Sandra. I happen to like babies and children. I've always wanted some of my own."

Sandra chuckled. "That's hard to believe, Wyatt. You've never even talked about wanting to be a husband, much less a father."

"That doesn't mean I haven't thought about it. I just haven't found the right woman."

She laughed again. "I guess that means I was never in the running."

He grimaced. "You and I both know you'd make an awful wife and mother, Sandra."

She groaned with good humor. "You're right. I'm a career woman. Period. But what about this Chloe Murdock? You haven't said that much about her. Does she seem like the mothering sort?"

Instead of the mountains, Wyatt was suddenly seeing Chloe's pale golden skin and deep red hair, the fierce look in her green eyes when he'd talked about taking the twins home with him. Yes, she was a mother at heart. It was the very thing about her that bothered him the most.

Later that evening, when Rose arrived at the Bar M to help Chloe with the evening chores, her thirteen-year-old stepdaughter, Emily, was with her.

The moment the girl stepped down from the pickup truck, Chloe gave her a tight, affectionate hug. "Don't tell me your mother is making you work this evening," Chloe teased. "You know, if you let her, she can be a real slave driver."

Emily cast Rose a loving smile. "No, she never makes me do anything. She always asks. But I volunteered this evening. I wanted to see for myself how Martin was doing."

Chloe waved a hand toward the calf's pen. "He's getting fat and slick and sassy. If you want to give him his supper, his bottle is in the feed room."

"I would!"

Emily hurried away, leaving the two sisters standing on the worn foot-path leading to the stable.

"Aunt Kitty called and told me all about Mr. Sanders," Rose said gravely. "Does Justine know?"

Chloe nodded. "I saw her this afternoon. She's going to have Roy run a check on him."

"What do you think she'll find?"

Ever since Chloe had left Justine's house, she'd been

asking herself the very same thing. "I'm afraid Roy won't find anything out of order."

"So the guy seems respectable."

Respectable? Chloe could think of a dozen other ways to describe the man. Cool, slick, insensitive and arrogant.

"On the surface," she told Rose. "But who knows, maybe we'll get lucky and he'll turn out to be a piece of trash."

"Chloe!" Rose gently scolded. "That's an awful thing to say."

Chloe started walking in the direction of the stable. Rose followed, her long legs easily keeping up with Chloe's shorter, quicker strides.

"Chloe, have you stopped to think that Adam and Anna are his relatives, too? It can't be easy for the man having his sister die a drug-related death. And in a facility for the criminally insane, to boot."

Chloe rolled her eyes at her sister. Like Justine, Rose was a beautiful woman. Tall and slender with long, wavy chestnut hair, she had a quiet gracefulness about her that Chloe had always admired. She was smart and strong and steady and Chloe had been thrilled a few months ago when she'd finally fallen in love and married. Yet there were times Chloe wanted to shake Rose's composure.

"Rose, surely you haven't forgotten the woman nearly killed you and Harlan!"

"I don't know that she was intentionally trying to kill us," Rose said thoughtfully. "There wasn't any way she could have known we were riding fence when she started that fire. I think her plans were simply to kill our cattle and destroy our pasture-land. Not murder us."

"You've too generous a heart, Rose," Chloe said with a groan.

Rose shrugged. "The woman is gone, Chloe. I guess I can afford to be a little forgiving."

Chloe's lips compressed to a grim line. "Well, her

brother isn't gone,'' she said. "And I have a feeling he's going to be a much more formidable foe than Belinda Waller ever was.''

Beneath the brim of her battered felt hat, Rose's pale green eyes grew wide with concern. "Why do you say that? Is the man deranged?''

"No. Wyatt Sanders isn't deranged. He's determined.''

And Chloe desperately dreaded the moment she would see him again.

The next afternoon, Chloe decided to give Kitty a break from baby-sitting and herself a chance to spend a bit of time with the twins away from the ranch. After spending all night and the bigger part of the morning worrying and wondering about Wyatt Sanders and his threat to take the twins, she hoped a drive into town would cheer her dismal thoughts.

The day was sunny and very warm for early September, just the sort of weather that made her want to forget about work and simply stare up at the blue New Mexican sky. Something Chloe rarely got to do these days.

Before her father, Tomas, had died, there had been at least five wranglers to help work the ranch. Now there were only herself and Rose and Rose's husband, Harlan, to see that everything got done.

Many nights Chloe lay awake too tired to sleep. During those times, she'd often thought about her father and how things had changed so drastically since his death. He'd not only left Chloe and her sisters with a pair of siblings, he'd left them very nearly broke. Chloe figured she should hate him for what he'd done, but she couldn't. Good or bad, he was her father and she'd loved him fiercely.

Was that how Wyatt Sanders felt about his sister? Chloe wondered as she drove herself and the twins west toward Ruidoso. Was he blind to Belinda's evil doings because she'd been his sister, or did he simply not know all the fear and damage she'd caused?

Whatever the case, Chloe wished she could be more forgiving, like Rose. She knew it wasn't healthy to hold on to her anger. But she feared if she ever let herself weaken toward Wyatt Sanders, he'd find her soft spot, then batter it until she finally surrendered.

No, the best way to handle Wyatt Sanders, she decided, was to be cool and steadfast.

Wyatt was in his car, traveling down Mechem Drive, when he spotted the redheaded woman pushing a double-seated baby stroller across the parking lot.

Even though she was wearing a skirt and her hair was pulled neatly to the back of her head, he could tell it was her. She had that quick, snappy walk that made her curves jiggle in a most feminine, distracting way.

Glancing in the rearview mirror, he jammed on the brakes and flipped on the turn signal. Chloe Murdock obviously hadn't come to town to see him, but she was going to, whether she liked it or not.

By the time Wyatt turned off the highway and parked the car, she was very nearly to the entrance of the grocery market. He called her name and she glanced over her shoulder. The moment she saw it was him she lifted her chin defensively.

"What do you want?" she asked as he drew within a few steps of her.

Wyatt shouldn't have been surprised by her blunt question. After all, yesterday he hadn't been all that congenial to her. But her coolness still managed to stop him in his tracks.

"I was driving down the street and happened to see you. I thought we might talk."

"I'm busy."

"I have a feeling you're always busy," he said, his eyes

making a quick search of her face. She had a touch of makeup on today, the soft pink color on her lips matched the color of her sweater. She looked so enchanting he found it difficult to remember she was the enemy.

"Your feeling is right."

Wyatt stepped to the front of the stroller for a better look at the twins. They were each dressed in bright printed T-shirts and denim overalls. The boy was wearing a baseball cap and the girl a floppy bonnet with a daisy pinned to the brim. Both children were mesmerized by the activity in the parking lot and paid little attention to him.

"Busy or not, Ms. Murdock, we're going to have to talk at some point in time." He lifted his gaze from the twins to look at her. "I'm a working man myself. I can't stay away from my office indefinitely." But he would stay as long as he could. As long as it took to make this woman see that the twins belonged in Houston where he could give them everything they needed.

"I'm glad to hear that," she said, then silently thanked God Rose wasn't here. Her sister hated it when Chloe was smart mouthed to anyone. "I'm sorry. I shouldn't have said that."

To Chloe's surprise, he smiled and as she took in the sexy curve of his lips, the white glint of his teeth and the crinkles at the corners of his gray eyes, she couldn't help but wonder what sort of man he might be under more normal circumstances.

"No, you shouldn't have," he agreed. "But then I said a lot to you yesterday that I probably shouldn't have, either. So we'll call things a draw."

Even though Chloe had a short temper fuse at times, she normally liked people and got on with them quite well. Maybe if she could put her anger aside for a while, she might be able to reason with this man. That was the first course Rose and Justine thought she should take. And what could simply talking to the man really hurt?

"I had planned to take the twins for ice cream after I finished buying groceries. If you'd like to meet us at Fred's in," she glanced at her wristwatch, "about twenty minutes from now, I could talk then."

It was much more than Wyatt expected to get from her and he wondered what had brought on the sudden change of heart. A moment ago, he could have sworn she was going to tell him to get lost or go talk to her lawyer.

"I'll be there. Where is it?"

"Just stay on this main thoroughfare." She inclined her head toward the street behind his shoulder. "Go down the mountain about three or four blocks toward the older part of town. Fred's is a small place on the left."

"Thank you, Ms. Murdock."

The sincerity in his voice and on his face took her by complete surprise and for a moment she didn't know what to say.

"No one calls me Ms. Murdock," she told him. "Please call me Chloe."

He smiled again and she felt her heart give a foolish little lurch.

"Okay, Chloe. I'll see you in twenty minutes."

She nodded in agreement, then pushed the stroller on toward the entrance of the grocery market. But for some crazy, unexplainable reason, it was a struggle for Chloe not to look over her shoulder and watch him walk back to his car.

Chapter Four

When Chloe entered Fred's a half hour later, Wyatt Sanders was already seated at a window booth which overlooked the encroaching woods at the back of the building.

As she and the twins approached the booth, he stood and said, "I see you made it. Thank you for coming."

He was smiling again, and that bothered Chloe. Mainly because it seemed so genuine and she wasn't quite ready to believe in this man's sincerity. "My shopping took a little longer than I anticipated. I hope you haven't been waiting long."

The smile deepened and Chloe felt an urgent need to draw a deeper breath.

"I have nothing else to do," he said, then looked down at the twins. "Where are the babies going to sit?"

Chloe glanced over her shoulder to a spot where the high chairs were usually stored. She was thankful there were two empty ones. "If you'll be kind enough to get a couple of those high chairs, we'll put them at the end of the table."

Wyatt fetched the chairs and Chloe quickly strapped

each baby inside. Both children seemed to know they were in store for a treat. They each squealed with excitement and pounded the trays across their laps with chubby hands.

Chloe had just taken a seat across from Wyatt when a waitress arrived. Chloe quickly ordered a hot fudge sundae for herself and a bowl of vanilla ice cream for the twins. Wyatt simply wanted coffee.

After the woman had left, Wyatt said, "I really do appreciate your meeting me like this. I know it's not something you particularly wanted to do."

No. Meeting Wyatt Sanders for any reason wasn't on her list of want-to-dos. But had she really had a choice in the matter?

"Whatever you might think, I'm not insensitive to the fact that the twins are your niece and nephew."

His dark brows rose with faint surprise. "Well, whatever you might think, the fact that I'm their uncle means a lot to me."

Her eyes connected with his and she felt a jolt rock her all the way down to her toes. "Your being here proves that to me," she said, then deliberately turned her attention to the twins, who were still making a loud but happy ruckus.

Wyatt was trying hard not to stare at the soft profile of her face, when she turned back to him and asked, "Have you ever been to this part of the state before?"

"No. I've done a lot of traveling in the past few years, some of it overseas, but I must admit I've never been here before."

The waitress appeared with their orders. After she'd placed them on the table and left, Wyatt went on, "Until I was notified of her death, I really had no idea my sister was in New Mexico. The last time I spoke to her, she told me she was in Vail, Colorado, and that she was planning on taking an extended vacation to Europe. That was over a year ago. Since then I tried contacting her at several of her old addresses, but I never heard a word.''

Like judging good horseflesh, Chloe could usually tell when a person was lying outright. In this case, she believed Wyatt was being entirely truthful.

Picking up a plastic spoon, she offered Anna a bite of the ice cream. Once the little girl had downed it, she did the same for Adam.

''Didn't that worry you?'' she asked Wyatt. ''Not hearing from Belinda at all?''

Shrugging, Wyatt sipped his coffee, then said, ''I wasn't particularly uneasy about it. You should understand that my sister was...well, you might say she was a free spirit of sorts.''

''You didn't see her often?''

He lowered his coffee cup onto the tabletop. ''Not after she divorced. She moved away from Houston and traveled from place to place. I think that helped her get over the break from her husband. At least that's what she implied.''

Chloe couldn't help but be intrigued by this man and the woman who had turned her father's head. ''But Vail and Europe? How could she live like that? I know my father was sending her money. But not that sort of money!''

It didn't take Wyatt but a moment to see what a chore it was to feed two babies at once. He motioned his head toward the bowl of ice cream.

''You're never going to get to take a bite of your sundae. Why don't you let me feed Adam?''

Him feed a baby? She shot him a skeptical look. ''Do you know how to feed a baby?''

His tanned face took on a ruddy tinge. ''Well, I haven't ever actually fed one, but it doesn't look that complicated. Just stick the spoon up to his mouth and let him do the rest.''

It was on the tip of Chloe's tongue to turn down his

offer. But for some reason, the idea struck her that it might do him good to see what caring for a baby, even in this small way, would be like.

Deliberately, she tucked more napkins around the neck of Adam's T-shirt and overall bib, then handed Wyatt another spoon. "Okay, you're welcome to give it a try," she told him.

Eager, but tentative, Wyatt scooped up a spoonful of ice cream and stuck it up to Adam's lips. At first the boy was so intrigued by the idea of being fed by a stranger, he merely stared, mouth closed, at Wyatt.

"What's the matter with him? He was eating fine for you."

Chloe kept a smug smile to herself. "He doesn't know you. Would you let a stranger poke something into your mouth?"

Wyatt frowned as he watched little Anna open her lips and smack the ice cream from Chloe's spoon.

"Okay, young man," he said to the cherub-faced little boy. "I'm your Uncle Wyatt. I'm not a stranger. It's perfectly safe to eat what I give you."

Adam cocked his head to one side, looked at his sister and Chloe, then burst out with a string of coos and giggles.

Wyatt lowered the spoon. "He thinks I'm funny."

Chloe chuckled softly. "He thinks you're different."

He glanced across the table at her. She was feeding herself now, digging the thick fudge off the bottom of the plastic bowl. Even though she ate daintily, he could see she was relishing every bite. It was a refreshing sight for Wyatt. Most of the women he knew considered picking at a plate of lettuce and bean sprouts to be eating a meal.

"Are the twins not used to being around men?" he asked.

"My brothers-in-law, Harlan and Roy, see the twins most everyday," she assured him, then motioned her head toward the spoon of melting ice cream in his hand. "Offer it to him again. He's had time to think about you now."

"All right, little buddy," he said to Adam. "Here it is. Don't just look at it. Eat it."

Adam complied this time and Wyatt breathed a sigh of relief. He was a grown man and he'd been assuring this woman the twins would be better off in his care. It wouldn't look good if he couldn't even manage to feed the baby a spoonful of ice cream.

"You were wondering about Belinda's finances," he began, as Adam continued to eat the ice cream from the spoon. "Well, at one time my sister had enough money to go to Europe or wherever she wanted."

"You say she had the money at one time. When was that?" she asked as she continued to feed Anna.

Chloe's question caused his features to tighten, but then Adam smacked his lips, and Wyatt looked at the baby and smiled.

"My father was an executive for a big petroleum firm in Houston. When he died, my sister and I inherited money and stocks. Enough to leave us both quite secure. I never worried or wondered if Belinda was squandering her part. When we talked, she always assured me her finances were doing fine. That she was doing fine. But now..." He let out a rueful sigh. "I don't know what happened. If she left any of the money or stock certificates somewhere in a bank, I can't find it."

"From what Roy—you remember I told you the sheriff is my brother-in-law?" Wyatt nodded and Chloe went on, "Well, Roy said it appeared to him that Belinda was barely scraping by. The last few places she'd lived in were... rattraps."

Wyatt shook his head. "I don't disbelieve your brother-in-law. I'm not going to dispute what he apparently saw firsthand. I just find it...incredible to think Belinda was broke. I realize she liked to travel and entertain. And she was never stingy when it came to her friends, but she wasn't stupid. I can't imagine her wasting all that money. It was her security.''

When Chloe had first agreed to meet with Wyatt, she hadn't necessarily expected to be discussing Belinda. She'd figured the only thing this man wanted to say to her was that he wanted the twins and meant to get them at any cost. But now, as she looked across the table and watched him awkwardly spooning ice cream into Adam's mouth, she could see a sadness in his eyes that told her he was a man alone. And that touched her more than anything he could have said.

"I wish there was something I could tell you," she said to him. "But you see, our father…well, we didn't know anything about Belinda. What little we do know about her is what she told the authorities. She said she met Daddy at the racetrack here at Ruidoso Downs.''

His lips twisted with wry fondness. "That sounds true enough. Belinda liked to play the horses.''

"So did Daddy." She absently dipped into her sundae as memories of Tomas welled up inside her. He'd been a big burly man full of humor and a zest for life. She hadn't known any other man who had loved horses as much as her father. Nor would she ever find a man who would love her as much as he had. The ache of missing him was still like a knife blade in her heart.

Glancing up at Wyatt, she asked, "Do you have a mother?''

Adam appeared to be full of ice cream. Wyatt put the spoon down and gently wiped the boy's mouth with the corner of a napkin.

"My mother left when I was very young.''

"Left? You mean she passed away?''

His handsome mouth twisted as though her question had left acid on his tongue. "No. I mean she left. Literally. Walked out and never came back.''

Even though Chloe had no reason to be embarrassed, she was. Splotches of red heat filled her cheeks.

"I shouldn't have asked. But since the twins' grandparents are gone on my side I was curious." She dipped her spoon into the melting sundae. "I guess not having grandparents isn't the end of the world." But having a mother desert you would be, Chloe thought sadly.

He sighed. "I suppose there might be ways of tracing my mother, but that could take years. And what would be the point? She didn't want me or Belinda. She certainly wouldn't be interested in grandchildren."

Dear God, were there really women in this world like that? Of course she'd heard stories on the news, but still it was so difficult for her to imagine any woman turning away from her own children.

"So it's been just you and Belinda? You don't have any other family?"

He shook his head. "My father was an only child. We never knew any of our mother's family."

She kept her eyes on the tabletop. "You're...uh, not married?"

He didn't answer immediately. Chloe glanced up to see a faint frown marring his forehead. "What's the matter? You're divorced?"

"No. I've never been married." He picked up his coffee cup. "I was just wondering why you asked."

Chloe shifted on the padded bench and wondered why her heart was behaving as if she'd just run a mile. "Because I...wondered if perhaps you had a wife back home who wanted the babies."

When Wyatt had first left Houston to drive out here to Hondo, he'd thought several times how much better it would be if he were married to a loving, nurturing woman he could take the babies home to. It would make much more of an argument for his case. But now, looking across the table at Chloe, he knew deep down he was glad he wasn't married. Which didn't make a bit of sense. He couldn't be looking at this woman as anything but a foe.

"Have you ever been married?" he asked her.

Three, even two, years ago that question would have filled Chloe's eyes with tears. Now it simply brought a caustic laugh to her lips. "No. I guess I'm just not...good marriage material."

He didn't know what she meant by that. And right now he couldn't care. He was here to get the twins. Nothing more. Nothing less.

Turning his gaze on the twins, who were presently entranced with three small children in the booth next to them, Wyatt said, "For the past ten years I've been busy getting my career off the ground. Then I turned thirty a few months ago and I began to realize how much I'd like to get married and have children."

Then why didn't he marry and have some of his own? Chloe wanted to ask. And leave her babies alone.

Wiping Anna's face with a napkin, she said, "You might as well know right now, I'm a frank person. What I say, I mean. There's no way on earth I'd give up the twins. I love them. They're my children and—"

Wyatt held up his hand. "At this point I know how you feel. I even respect you for it. But—and I'm saying this not for myself, but for the twins—you need to stop and consider the difference I could make in their lives."

Chloe did her best to remember Justine and Rose's advice to hang on to her temper. "Like I said, I won't give up the twins, but let's just say for instance that I did. How would you take care of them? You have a job. You couldn't be mommy and daddy to them all the time."

"I have plenty of money to hire a nanny while I'm away."

She arched one brow at him. "You think a nanny can replace family?"

He shot her a dry look. "They're two little babies. They don't know who's related to them."

She groaned. "You just don't get it, do you?"

"What?"

"You don't understand what it means to have a family around you," she answered.

He looked insulted. "I had a family. At one time in my life."

"You had a mother and father. A sister. But were you all a family?"

His gray eyes were suddenly the color of blue steel. "Do you mean, did we all sit down together at breakfast for a bowl of cornflakes every morning? Or watch 'Lassie' together every Sunday evening?"

What was it about this man? Chloe wondered. How could he make her feel so infuriated and so torn all at once? He was full of sarcasm, and she wanted to tell him how superficially he viewed life. Yet she also wanted to give and show him the kindness, the closeness she knew he desperately needed.

"That wasn't really what I meant," she said, then made an impatient swipe through the air with her hand. "And since you don't understand, I'll try to explain it this way. I'd much rather the twins be watching 'Lassie' on Sunday evening with their family than worrying over how to fatten their bank accounts."

"From the look of things, it wouldn't hurt you and your sisters to do a little worrying."

He could have said anything but that. For months Chloe had lain awake at nights wondering where the ranch's next dollar would come from and how it was going to cover everything her family needed to live. And his sister had put them in this desperate situation!

Acid words burned her tongue, but she kept them to herself as she stood and quickly began to unbuckle the babies from their high chairs.

"What are you doing?"

"I'm going home."

His eyes roamed her flushed face. "I've made you angry."

She let out a dry little laugh as she lifted Anna from the chair and placed her into the stroller. Once she'd straightened from her task, she looked Wyatt square in the eyes. "I know all about having money and not having money. Your sister took all of ours away. But you know, I still think I'm far richer than you'll ever be."

In that instant Wyatt knew he wasn't dealing with just any woman. Chloe Murdock wasn't typical or gullible or easily impressed. She wasn't like any woman he'd ever known. So how did he ever expect to get through to her?

Without a backward glance, she pushed the stroller out of the little café and headed toward her pickup. She was only a few steps away from the door when Wyatt's hand came down on her forearm. She whirled on him, her green eyes flashing with outrage.

"What are you doing?" she asked, glancing pointedly to where his fingers snared her arm.

"I'm sorry. I shouldn't have said that to you back there."

She told herself not to look at him, but her eyes betrayed her. "Forget it. It's ridiculous for us to think we could talk civilly about anything. We're on opposite sides."

"No. That's where you're wrong. We both want what's best for the twins, don't we?"

She contemplated his question for a moment, then nodded. "I hope you really mean that."

"I do."

Most of her anger faded as quickly as it had flared. Yet she moved toward the pickup anyway. It was time for her to go home and get away from this man.

"Chloe?"

With Adam cradled in her arms, she glanced at him. "Yes?"

"Did my sister really take all your money?"

She could see he was appalled by the very idea. And she couldn't help thinking the Murdock family weren't the only ones Belinda had duped.

Chloe gave one rueful nod of her head. "Once the ranch account was depleted, Daddy borrowed several thousand dollars from Harlan. He wasn't Rose's husband then. Just a friend and neighbor. But he loaned Daddy the money, accepting the Bar M as collateral. All of that money went to Belinda, too."

Dear Lord, what had his sister been thinking? What was she doing with the money and why would she have wanted to take from these people? She'd had so much of her own.

"Then technically the ranch belongs to your brother-in-law, Harlan?"

Chloe frowned at him. "There's no technically about it. After he and Rose married, he was generous enough to dissolve the loan. You see, there is no yours or mine in our family. It's strictly ours."

One corner of his mouth cocked upward. "I've always heard it was bad business to be partners with family members."

She gave him a weary look. "We're not talking about business here, Wyatt. We're talking about our home."

Not wanting to let things go at that, Wyatt followed as she pushed the stroller to the pickup.

Chloe opened the door, then turned around to retrieve the twins from their stroller.

"Oh!" She gasped as her face nearly collided with Wyatt's chest. "I didn't know you were back there."

Amused by her surprise, Wyatt's eyes took their time going over every feature of her face. "There was something else I wanted to talk to you about."

He was standing so close she could see the pores in his

dark skin, the granite flecks radiating out from his pupils and the uneven line of his very white teeth. The wind had ruffled his black hair, sending two straight locks spilling over his forehead. The faintest hint of sandalwood and musk emanated from his pale blue shirt, reminding Chloe even more of his maleness.

"Don't you think we've already said it all?"

A faint smile touched his face. "I wanted to see if it would be okay with you if I came out to the ranch again tomorrow."

"To see the twins?"

"And you."

Chloe wasn't exactly sure what he meant by that and for the moment she was too unsettled to ask.

"Well, since I haven't persuaded you to pack your bags and head back to Houston—yet—I guess I could do it over supper tomorrow night. If plain old ranch grub will be all right with you."

Supper with Chloe and her family? It wasn't what Wyatt had in mind. He wanted to be on this woman's good side, but that didn't mean he wanted or needed to rub elbows with her. Still, the invitation was too good to turn down for any reason.

"I'll be there. What time?"

"Six or so. No, better make it seven. The farrier is coming tomorrow afternoon and sometimes one or two of the horses give him a bad time and it takes him longer than expected to finish."

"I can't imagine *you* having a temperamental horse."

She gave him a provocative smile. "It would be boring if everything and everyone bent to my will, now wouldn't it?"

If she wasn't flirting with him, she was getting damn close. The idea excited Wyatt in spite of his intentions to remain distant.

"I believe you'll find I don't bend very easily, Chloe."

No. She didn't imagine he complied to anyone's wishes. Unless he wanted to.

Ducking beneath the arm he'd propped on the pickup door, she lifted Anna out of the stroller.

Turning to help her, Wyatt lifted Adam out of the stroller and into his arms. The boy immediately grabbed for Wyatt's chin and hung on with a healthy grip.

"I guess he's checking out my shaving ability," Wyatt joked, surprised at how much the baby's soft little hand affected him.

Back in Houston, Wyatt hadn't expected to feel instant love for the twins. Even though they were his sister's children, he hadn't even known they'd existed until a few short weeks ago when he'd been contacted about Belinda's death.

The twins were strangers to him. And yet he couldn't deny that yesterday when he'd walked into the Bar M kitchen, the sight of the babies had gone straight to his heart. And now, holding Adam and feeling the baby's hand exploring his face, he knew that coming here had been the right thing to do. The twins needed him. And if Wyatt wanted to be totally honest with himself, he needed the twins.

"Babies like to touch what they see."

She reached for Adam and Wyatt reluctantly handed him over to her.

"That must prove troublesome at times."

Her expression bemused, she asked, "Have you never been around babies before?"

"No. But I plan to remedy that in the coming days."

She raised her eyebrows but said nothing as she turned and placed Adam into the car seat beside his sister. Her fingers fumbled several times before she finally managed to secure the seat belts across both children. All the while she could feel Wyatt just behind her shoulder. Waiting for what, she didn't know. She only knew he was playing havoc with her senses.

"I'd better be getting home. Aunt Kitty wasn't expecting me to be gone this long," she told him. "She'll be worried if I don't show up soon."

He wanted to tell her she should have a cellular phone in her truck, especially traveling with the children over a twenty-mile stretch of desert mountain highway. But he stopped himself short. Chloe Murdock couldn't afford a cellular phone. Was that really Belinda's fault? Was this woman having to struggle to make ends meet because of his sister's reckless behavior? He didn't want to think so. But even if it were true, he didn't owe Chloe anything. Did he?

He stepped back so she could shut the door.

"Drive carefully," he said.

She skirted the cab of the truck and climbed behind the wheel. "I'm always careful with the children."

He hadn't been thinking only of the twins' safety. He'd been thinking of her, too. Thank goodness, she didn't know that. The last thing he needed was for Chloe Murdock believing she'd gotten under his skin.

Chapter Five

"This is totally unnecessary," Chloe said to her sisters the next evening as they both attempted to shoo her out of the stable.

"We'll finish up here," Rose assured her. "You go on to the house and get ready for your dinner guest."

"Dinner guest. Hell's bells, Rose! Belinda Waller's brother isn't my dinner guest!"

Justine rolled her eyes. "Well, the man is coming to supper, Chloe. What else would you call him?"

Chloe could think of several choice words, but she knew her sisters, especially Rose, wouldn't appreciate hearing them.

Turning to Justine, she said, "You shouldn't even be down here. Roy will have a fit if he finds out!"

"Roy knows exactly where I am and what I'm doing. The doctor wants me to get exercise and I won't lift anything I shouldn't. Rose will make sure of that."

Seeing she couldn't argue with either of them, Chloe threw up her hands and headed out of the stable.

"Chloe, please hold on to your temper and be nice to the man," Rose called after her.

"Remember," Justine added, "sugar catches more flies than vinegar."

"Who's going to be doing any fly catching? I just want to make the man see he's wasting his time here."

Up at the house Chloe found Kitty already busy in the kitchen. When she spotted several New York strips lying on the butcher block, she asked in a scandalized voice, "You're not going to fix these, are you? These are the ranch's best steaks! We only eat these on special occasions."

Kitty shrugged as she cut shortening into a bowl of flour. "This is a special occasion. The twins' uncle is coming for dinner."

Just hearing Kitty say the word *uncle* chilled her. "You make it sound like he's already a part of the family!"

Kitty pointed the pastry blender at her niece. "Chloe, I think you need to face the fact that Wyatt Sanders will always be Adam and Anna's uncle. No matter what."

"I can live with that as long as he stays in Houston and the twins stay here," she said.

With a helpless shake of her head, Kitty turned back to her pastry bowl. "Do you mean to tell me that you'd like it if the twins never saw him?"

Sighing, Chloe walked over to the refrigerator and pushed a glass under the water dispenser on the door. "Would that be so bad?"

"Chloe, I'd be the first one to put up a fight if Wyatt tried to take the twins from this ranch. I don't think he should even consider trying to do such a thing. But I also believe it would be wrong of us to try to cut him totally out of their lives. He has a right to his family. Just like we do."

And the twins were the only family Wyatt had now, Chloe couldn't help thinking. For his sake, she regretted that. Everybody needed family. Including Wyatt Sanders. But he was a young, handsome man. He could marry and have children of his own. Chloe couldn't. As far as she was concerned that was the gist of the matter.

"You're probably right, Aunt Kitty. And don't worry, I'm going to politely invite Wyatt to be the twins' uncle. But not their father!"

She drained the glass of water and left the kitchen before Kitty could say more.

By seven that evening, Chloe was dressed in a pair of black silk pants and a red mohair sweater. Her hair was brushed loosely on her shoulders and tucked behind her ears, to which she'd clipped rhinestone teardrops.

She was still trying to decide if she was overdressed when she heard Wyatt's car pull up in front of the house. Glancing one last time in the mirror, she assured herself that anything more than jeans would look dressed up for her. Besides, Wyatt Sanders opinion of her looks mattered nothing whatsoever.

But a few moments later as she opened the door for him, her heart was pattering like a schoolgirl's on prom night.

"Good evening, Wyatt," she greeted while gesturing for him to come in. "You timed your arrival just right. Aunt Kitty is about to take the rolls out of the oven."

He stepped into a living room furnished with comfortable leather furniture. Throw rugs woven in bright southwestern patterns were scattered over the Spanish tiled floor. At one end of the room a small fire was burning in a rock fireplace.

Smells of good cooking reached his nose, but they didn't quite drown out the exotic scent of Chloe. Nor did his hunger pains divert his attention from the sight of her.

The deep red of her sweater suited her coloring, and the black pants, though loose and fluttery, still allowed him a glimpse of a voluptuous figure.

Suddenly remembering the wine in his hands, he thrust the bottle at her. "I didn't know what to bring." He'd been tempted to purchase a bouquet of fresh-cut flowers, but had quickly censured the idea. He wasn't Chloe's dinner date. He wasn't even her friend. "I hope some of your family likes burgundy."

"We all like wine," she assured him. "Thank you."

"It's already getting cool outside, but it feels good in here," he said, glancing once again at the welcoming fire.

"The twins like to crawl in this room before bedtime, and I didn't want the floor to be cold." She motioned toward the couch. "Have a seat and I'll go see if Aunt Kitty needs any help."

"Where are the twins? In the kitchen?"

Chloe nodded and he said, "Then I'd like to come with you and say hello."

"Suit yourself."

He followed her down a long hallway. At the end and to the right were a pair of wide, batwing doors. Chloe pushed through them and Wyatt found himself in the kitchen he'd been in two days ago.

Like then, the room was warm and full of the smells of cooking. The stacks of dirty dishes were gone as was the ironing board, but it was still very cluttered compared to his own kitchen.

At the sound of their footsteps, Kitty looked up from the salad she was tossing. "Hello, Mr. Sanders," she greeted.

Wyatt went over to the woman and offered her his hand. "Hello, Ms.—I don't believe I caught your last name the other day."

She wiped her hand on the front of her apron, then reached to shake Wyatt's. "No one ever uses my last name. Just call me Kitty."

"And I'd like you to call me Wyatt, if you would."

"Certainly. And if I seemed rude the other day, I hope

you'll forgive me. Learning the twins had an uncle just about floored me. It wasn't anything personal against you."

He waved away her words. "You have nothing to apologize for. This whole thing is—an unusual set of circumstances."

That was definitely an understatement, Chloe thought. She placed the bottle of wine on the cabinet counter. "Wyatt followed me to the kitchen to say hello to the twins," she told her aunt.

Kitty motioned to the other side of the room. "They're in their playpen."

Wyatt looked over to where a playpen had been wedged between a chest-type deep freeze and a Formica kitchen table. The twins were sitting up, facing each other. Scattered around them on the floor of the playpen were several cans of vegetables, a small cooking pot with a lid and a number of spoons and rubber spatulas. At the moment, Adam was banging one of the spatulas on everything within his reach, including his sister.

Walking over to the playpen, Wyatt squatted down on his heels to the babies' level. "Don't the twins have any toys?" he asked.

Chloe snorted while Kitty laughed and said, "Just a whole nursery full. But babies get bored with toys pretty fast. They like grown-up things to play with."

"I hope that doesn't include knives and guns."

"We're not crazy," Chloe said sharply.

"Chloe! Wyatt was only teasing," Kitty admonished her niece.

He hadn't been teasing, exactly. But he was glad Kitty had thought so. He didn't want to be insulting. It was just that these people lived so differently from him and he didn't know anything about babies. Being ignorant left him saying things he was constantly wanting to take back.

Walking over to the playpen, Chloe looked down at him. "Were you teasing?"

It seemed all they could do was ruffle each other's feathers, Wyatt thought. Which was a puzzle to him. Usually he didn't have any problem dealing with women. "I know you don't let the children play with anything dangerous," he assured her.

Somewhat mollified, Chloe held out her arms toward the two babies. "Okay little darlings, show Uncle Wyatt how you can stand up all by yourselves."

Like typical children, when asked to show off their achievements the twins refused to cooperate.

Wyatt smiled. "They don't seem to mind you too well."

She grimaced. "They're too young to mind anyone."

"Can they walk? When will they have teeth?"

So he truly didn't know about babies or toddlers. It made her wonder why he would want to take on the enormous task of raising two. Surely there was more to it than just wanting to help his late sister.

"Some babies walk at nine months, some are much older. Adam and Anna are trying. They can stand with just a little bit of help now. As for their teeth, they each have five."

"Five teeth!" He appeared surprised and impressed. "Then they can chew regular food?"

"A few soft things. They still take a bottle and will for a couple of more months."

"Chloe, everything is ready if you want to help me carry things into the dining room," Kitty spoke up behind them.

Wyatt straightened to his full height. "There's no need to do that for me. We could eat here in the kitchen, unless you have more people coming and need the room."

"There's no one else coming for dinner," Chloe assured him. "My sisters and their families were busy tonight." Deliberately she could have added. For some reason she couldn't fathom, they had all agreed it would be better if she negotiated with Wyatt by herself, rather than throw a whole army of family at him.

"Are you sure?" Kitty asked him. "We have a nice dining room. We don't use it too often except when company, or more of the family comes."

Well, Wyatt was neither company nor family. Worse than that, he knew he wasn't really wanted here. They were tolerating him, welcoming him into their home because he'd practically left them no choice. And suddenly, as he took in the babies and Chloe, Kitty and the warm, cluttered kitchen, he wished it wasn't that way. He wished he wasn't someone they feared and resented.

"Eating here in the kitchen will be fine with me. Can I do anything to help?"

Neither Chloe nor Kitty was used to a man's help in the kitchen. While he was living, Tomas had avoided the room. The only thing Harlan and Roy were good at was opening a can and heating the contents. And that was only when they had to. Wyatt's offer had both women staring at him with disbelief.

"I do know my way around the kitchen," he assured them. "I've cooked for myself for years."

The last thing Chloe had expected him to be tonight was amicable. It made her wonder if he was merely trying to butter them up. Or did he actually want to be helpful? How could she know? How could she trust him about anything?

"I'll help Aunt Kitty carry the food to the table. You might open the wine you brought," she suggested.

Smiling to himself, Wyatt went to fetch the wine bottle from the cabinet counter. Chloe might not want him here, but little by little she was bending. Maybe after a few more days he'd have her changing her mind about a lot of things.

Moments later they sat down to steak, wilted salad, baked potatoes and hot rolls. Between bites for herself, Chloe fed Adam and Anna mashed baked potatoes.

"The babies usually have their meal a little earlier than

we do," Kitty told Wyatt. "But Chloe always likes to feed them a bit of table food when we eat."

"They like it better than that pureed stuff," Chloe explained.

"Well, pretty soon you're going to have them so spoiled they'll be spitting out the baby food and crying for meat and potatoes."

Chloe made an exaggerated happy face at both twins and the babies giggled loudly. "That's okay. Justine said I could put most any sort of meat in the blender and break it down to a consistency they can eat."

Wyatt thought he remembered Justine being the name of the woman who'd found the babies on the front porch. "Justine is your sister?"

"She's the middle one of us," Chloe answered.

"She and Roy Pardee married back in the early part of July so she doesn't live on the ranch anymore," Kitty explained.

Chloe added, "She has a five-year-old son and another child on the way. She's also a nurse, so she knows all about caring for children."

Wyatt tried to digest all this information. "Then her son is from a former marriage?"

Kitty shook her head, while Chloe wondered why he was bothering to learn about her family. If she would agree to let him take the twins, he'd be gone from here in the wink of an eye and never think twice about any of the Murdocks.

"No. Charlie is Roy's son. Roy just didn't know about Charlie for a while. And for a while Justine believed he didn't want to know about him," Kitty told him, then waved her fork through the air. "It's a long, complicated story. Maybe Chloe will tell you about it sometime."

Wyatt glanced curiously at Chloe. "So both your sisters have married recently. That hasn't made you get the itch for a husband?"

Her expression unmoving, she said, "When I get an itch I get out the calamine lotion. I don't go looking for a man."

Kitty made a production of clearing her throat. "Chloe vows she'll never marry."

Chloe cast her aunt a look that warned her to go no further with explanations.

As Wyatt sliced off a bite of steak, he glanced at Chloe. "Is that so?"

Unconsciously lifting her chin, she said, "I told you. I'm not good marriage material. I have a mind of my own and I've found my horses make far better companions than men."

Though her statement intrigued him, he didn't probe further. Instead, he turned his attention to his food and tried to tell himself Chloe Murdock was just another beautiful woman, like any beautiful woman back in Houston. She just happened to have a stronger effect on him, that's all.

Kitty had prepared cherry cobbler for dessert. They had it with their coffee in the living room, while the twins crawled on the floor and pulled up to anything they could get their little hands on.

Several times Chloe had to get up to tend to them. As Wyatt watched her, he wondered where she found the energy to work at the stable all day, then chase after two rambunctious babies at night.

When the twins finally wore themselves down and began to whine and fuss, Kitty announced she was going to put them and herself to bed.

Chloe got up from the couch to help her, but the older woman quickly waved her back down. "No. I can manage. You stay here and visit with Wyatt. He might like another bowl of cobbler."

Groaning, Wyatt rubbed his midsection. "I couldn't eat another bite, Kitty. But thank you. It was all delicious."

It had been a long time since Chloe had seen such a

beaming smile on her aunt's face. And the fact that Wyatt Sanders put it there perplexed her. Kitty wasn't a fool where men were concerned. She knew they could turn on the charm whenever it suited their purpose. So what was the woman thinking?

After Kitty and the twins had disappeared down the hallway to the bedrooms, Chloe went over to the fireplace and tossed another log on the fire.

"I like your aunt. She's a very kind woman," Wyatt said as he sipped the last of his coffee. "How long has she lived here with you?"

"Several years. When my mother first became ill she moved in to be with her. To give her emotional support mainly. As sisters they were very close. Then after mother died we encouraged Aunt Kitty to stay with us. I think she needed us as much as we needed her."

"She's never been married or had a family of her own?"

Chloe shook her head as she held her hands toward the warmth of the fire. "Aunt Kitty was once involved with a married man. When that relationship ended, so did her interest in men."

The flatness of Chloe's voice bothered him. As did Kitty's earlier remark about Chloe never wanting to marry. She was a very young woman. Probably no more than twenty-five. And her beauty was the kind that turned a man's insides to hot mush. In Houston she could easily find a rich man to marry, one who would take her away from this drudgery. So why didn't she leave? What was holding her here?

"That's too bad. Kitty would make some man a good wife."

"I'm sure of it," Chloe agreed. "But sometimes life deals us an entirely different hand from what we hope for."

And what had she hoped for? Wyatt wondered. She

seemed contented with what she had. "To be honest, before I left Houston to come here, I figured you and your sisters would be glad for me to take the twins off your hands."

It was a good thing she didn't have a riding quirt in her hand, otherwise she would have been tempted to hit him with it. "You thought we wouldn't want our own brother and sister? How could you?"

"I figured you each had your own lives to worry about. And," he went on sheepishly, "I thought you would probably hold the circumstances of the twins' birth against them."

She didn't try to keep her mouth from falling open. "Dear God, what sort of women do you think we are? Just because your mother and sister didn't want children doesn't mean all women are that way! And especially Murdock women!"

His eyes narrowed. "I'll admit my mother wasn't a candidate for the cover of a parents' magazine. But you can't know that Belinda didn't want her babies!"

Chloe knew what she'd said to him was a low blow and she was a little regretful. But damn him, he was saying some pretty insulting things himself.

"She left the twins without a word. And when Roy arrested her she told him she hadn't wanted the babies. She had left them at the ranch thinking Daddy was still alive and she was leaving them with him." Closing her eyes for a moment, she shook her head, "Dear God, Daddy had already been dead for two months."

"Maybe it does look bad on her part," Wyatt countered. "But I know Belinda cared about her babies. Otherwise she wouldn't have written to me, asking me to come get them."

Chloe's green eyes widened. "She did that?"

"It's the main reason I'm here. She wanted me to be the twins' father."

"I find that hard to believe. The woman never mentioned your name."

"And I find it even more difficult to believe Belinda took all that money from your father!"

Before he knew it, Chloe's hand was wrapped around his wrist, tugging him up from the couch.

"What are you doing?"

"I want you to come with me."

He got up from the couch and she led him down the hallway and into a room that would have been dark if it hadn't been for the shafts of moonlight slanting through the windows.

Wyatt knew he should have his thoughts on what she was about to show him. But where Chloe Murdock was concerned, his mind had a will of its own. He was keenly aware of the touch of her hand, the scent of her perfume, the closeness of her body.

"If this is something to do with the money—"

"Don't say anything," she interrupted. "Yet."

Dropping his hand, she went to a large desk and switched on a banker's lamp. It shed a small pool of light on the desktop but did little to illuminate the room.

"This is where my father did all the ranch's bookkeeping. He also used this room as a place to relax and read. He was an educated man and could have taught school if he'd chosen to use his teaching degree, but he was an outdoorsman at heart and decided to build this ranch when he was younger than I am now."

"Which is?"

"Twenty-four."

She glanced at him from beneath her thick lashes, and not for the first time tonight, she noticed what a handsome man he was. Beneath his white shirt and dark olive trousers, he was broad shouldered, long legged and lean. She didn't know if the exercise he got was natural or forced, but either way he was obviously fit. Too fit for her peace of mind.

"That's very young to build a cattle empire."

"Daddy wasn't your everyday kind of man. He was special."

He studied her quiet face. "Then you don't hate him for the trouble he's caused the family?"

She looked down at the desktop to the ink blotter where Tomas's scribbled notes were still legible. To one side lay the same ledger where he'd posted his profits. And he had made plenty of profits in his day. She could still hear his laughter, smell his cigarette smoke—and she ached to have him back.

"Hate him? Never. I just can't understand what happened to him. Maybe it was seeing mother go like she did. Little by little until she was hardly more than a wisp of skin and bones. There was no doubt that he loved her fiercely. When she died he said his soul had gone with her. And sometimes I believe that might have been true."

Though he wanted to say something comforting, Wyatt was at a loss as to what it would be. And being who he was, he wasn't sure she would even accept sympathy from him.

Pushing her memories aside, Chloe bent down and pulled out a drawer at the bottom of the desk. Once she straightened, she handed Wyatt a thick white envelope.

"What is this?"

"Take a look," she urged.

He opened the envelope and pulled out a stack of checks bound with a heavy rubberband. For several minutes he sifted through them, studying the dates, the amounts and the account number stamped on the back.

After a while he bound the rubberband back around them, stuffed them in the envelope and handed them back to Chloe. "That is a lot of money," he said grimly.

Chloe nodded. "Those checks are what finally led Roy

to your sister. Before then we had no idea who the twins' mother was or that Daddy was the father.''

''Was there any money left in her bank account when Roy investigated?''

Chloe shook her head. ''By then she'd withdrawn it all and left town. The bank manager told Roy it had been a small amount.''

He let out a heavy sigh. ''What was she doing with all her money? The money your father had already sent her was more than enough to keep her adequately housed, fed and clothed.''

''We think she was simply blackmailing Daddy, threatening to tell us about her and the twins if he didn't pay. You can't deny she had a drug problem. The doctor said it was the reason her heart stopped so suddenly.''

Chloe was painting a picture of Belinda that was difficult for Wyatt to fathom and yet he had to face the fact that something had gone terribly wrong in his sister's life. Why hadn't he made a point to keep in touch with her? Why hadn't he been around to see what was happening and stop it?

''I had no idea Belinda had taken any sort of drugs until the doctors at the hospital explained her death to me. She'd had a slight heart murmur all her life and she'd been warned that alcohol or drugs would cause damage, so she knew the consequences. It all makes me wonder if she was slowly trying to kill herself. Especially if your father had rejected her.''

For the first time since all of this had happened, Chloe forced herself to look at things from Belinda's side. Had Tomas broken her heart and left her deserted with two little babies? No, she didn't think so. Belinda herself had admitted that Tomas had wanted the children. And then there was all that money he'd sent her. That had to mean something.

''I don't know what she was thinking or what was on

Daddy's mind. We'll probably never know. But one thing is for certain—their affair has left the Bar M drained."

He looked at her. "That's all the more reason you should want the twins to live with me. Rather than here in poverty."

Her nostrils flaring, she shoved the canceled checks back in the drawer and closed it. "I hardly think we live in poverty," she said tightly.

"Maybe not. But you might be, soon."

She couldn't believe his gall or his priorities. "And whose fault is that?" she countered hotly.

So now they were finally getting to the point, he thought with angry disappointment. Up until now, Chloe had done a good job of putting on an air of family pride, but when it came right down to the gist of things, she was like all the rest.

"I guess the next thing you're going to say is that if I were a real man, I'd offer you financial help to raise the twins rather than take them with me?"

Thinking it was high time to leave the room, she reached over and switched off the lamp. "I wouldn't take a dime from you! And neither would the rest of my family! Your sister whammed us hard, but we will come back from it. And no thanks to you!"

Chloe's reaction to his question surprised him more than anything yet. In his life, money was always a bargaining chip. And because he had lots of it, he'd often been approached for loans and handouts. In his younger years, he'd been softhearted and allowed friends, many of them women, to use him for their financial gain.

He supposed having money had caused him to become jaded about human nature. But he'd learned it was foolish to trust anyone. Especially beautiful women like Chloe.

She brushed past him and headed toward the door. Wyatt quickly snagged a hold on her shoulder and spun her back to him. "Do you mean you'd have the twins suffer because of your pride?"

She tried to jerk free of his grip, but he only tightened his hold. "Suffer?" she repeated inanely. "You think the twins would suffer living here?"

He rolled his eyes. "Come on, Chloe. Look around you. This isolated ranch has nothing to offer them. I could afford to give them the best of care. Private schools, any college they chose. In Houston, I could open doors to successful careers for them. They would be exposed to fine art and culture. They'd know more about life than cows and horses and sagebrush and cactus."

This was the point where Chloe should have been exploding with anger. But oddly she wasn't. She was sad for Wyatt Sanders. And torn. Because she could think of nothing she might say or do that would make him understand what was lacking in his scheme of things.

"I won't waste my breath telling you we Murdocks know a little bit more than cows and horses. But I would like to ask one important thing."

"Yes?"

"You tell me if you had the twins they would get the best of schools, colleges and careers. They would have the opportunity to make plenty of money. But will they be loved?"

His nostrils flared with indignation. "How could you ask such a thing?"

"It wasn't hard. I just opened my mouth and—"

His hands suddenly gripped both her shoulders. "How dare you imply that I wouldn't love the twins."

She tilted her head back and glared at him. "I dare because I don't think you have any idea what the word really means. Your world revolves around money and very little else. What could you know about loving another human being?"

His gray eyes took on a strange glitter and then suddenly

his face became a blur and his breath whispered hot against her lips.

"You definitely are a smart-mouthed little thing," he muttered.

Much to Chloe's dismay, her knees went weak, her breathing shallow. She didn't want to be this close to him. Yet she was powerless to step back.

"I'm not a little *thing*. Especially to you."

Wyatt could stand it no longer. He had to kiss her, had to prove to her that he wasn't just an oil tycoon. He was a man who needed, loved and hurt.

As soon as his lips settled over hers, Chloe knew she was in trouble. Her stomach fluttered, her heart stilled and heat poured through her veins. She'd been kissed before. Plenty of times, but she couldn't ever remember it feeling like this.

Loosening the grip on her shoulders, Wyatt slid his arms around her back and pulled her up against him. Through the softness of her sweater, he could feel the thrust of her firm breasts, the narrow indention of her waist and the hardness of her thighs. She tasted sweet and giving. Nothing like the acid words she'd spat at him, and Wyatt couldn't help but want to go on exploring this soft, feminine side of her.

When Wyatt finally decided to end the kiss, Chloe was totally breathless. For long moments she could do nothing more than stand there, her eyes closed, her senses scattered.

In the dim moonlight, Wyatt could see the faint quiver of her bottom lip, the throb of her pulse at the side of her neck. Hair was tangled over one eye and her lashes lay like dark little wings against her pale skin. She looked far too sexy for any one man to bear. Yet there was a vulnerableness about her face that made him want simply to draw her head against his chest, hold her tightly to him until all her fears and doubts had quieted.

Wyatt had never felt such desire, such fierce protectiveness for anyone in his life, and the realization stunned him.

Turning away from her, he said, "I'm...sorry about that."

So was Chloe. Sorry that she'd liked it. Sorry that for those few moments in his arms she'd felt like a real woman again.

She swallowed, then said, "Don't apologize. You got your point over."

Wyatt turned back to her, his eyes narrowed with skepticism. "You think I was trying to make a point?"

She nodded while thinking how strange it was to be so cool and distant from him now when only a few moments ago she'd been so close and warm in his arms.

"You're a man. Not a bank account."

She was so on target with his feelings, he was momentarily taken aback. In the past, he'd dated women for months at a time and none of them had ever picked up the message. Chloe had gotten it after one kiss. The whole idea shook him like the gale of a windstorm.

"That's right," he said more gruffly than he intended. "And you'll do well to remember it. Now I think it's time for me to go."

He brushed past her and Chloe stood where she was. It would be better to let him find his own way out, she thought.

And she hoped he'd soon find his way back to Houston. Without the twins. And without her heart.

Chapter Six

The next morning, Chloe looked up from her seat in the medical clinic waiting room to see Rose and Justine hurrying toward her.

"What happened?" Rose questioned.

"How is she?" Justine wanted to know.

The two women took seats on the plastic chairs next to Chloe. She waited until they were settled, then answered Rose's question first.

"I don't know exactly how it happened, and I don't think Aunt Kitty does either. It was before daylight and I'd been down at the stable feeding. On the way back to the house for breakfast I found Aunt Kitty in the yard trying to hobble on one leg back to the porch. She'd been carrying out the trash and stepped in a hole or something and fell. It's a miracle she didn't bust her head wide open. You know how rocky the ground is around the trash barrel."

"Was she able to walk at all?" Justine asked, aghast.

Chloe shook her head. "Not really. Dr. Bellamy thinks her ankle is broken. They're taking X rays right now."

"Where are the twins?" Rose asked, noticing for the first time that the two babies weren't anywhere in the waiting room.

"Vida, Aunt Kitty's friend, came over to watch them while I drove her to the doctor."

The three women fell into a worried silence. Finally Justine said, "If Aunt Kitty's ankle is truly broken, she's going to be out of action for a long while. Someone will have to help you with the twins, Chloe."

Sighing, Chloe slumped against the back of the uncomfortable chair. Finding Kitty injured and in so much pain had taken the starch out of her. She already felt as if she'd done two days' work when actually the morning wasn't even over yet.

"I know. That's already crossed my mind. And what a time for this to happen," she said with a groan.

"What do you mean?" Rose asked, "Anytime would be bad."

"I know," Chloe agreed. "But with Wyatt Sanders here, he's going to be poking his nose in things. He'll probably say it's a good time for him to take the twins to Houston because I won't be able to care for them."

Justine said with a wave of her hand, "Don't be ridiculous. We'll shift things around so some of us can take care of the twins during the day. I could do it part of the time."

Chloe instantly shook her head. "You're in no condition to be chasing after two babies!"

"Chloe is right," Rose spoke up. "We know you want to help, Justine, but you've got your own unborn baby to think about. It would be exhausting for you to take care of the twins for two hours much less all day."

Justine rolled her eyes at her sisters. "Girls, I'm as healthy as a horse."

"And that's the way we want to keep you," Chloe

countered, then added, "Speaking of kids, where's Charlie?"

Smiling at the mention of her son's name, Justine said, "He's riding around with his daddy in the sheriff's car. They're going to pick me up in a little while."

Another silence fell between the sisters as more people came and went in the waiting room. After a while Rose glanced at her youngest sister, "So tell us how things went last night with Wyatt Sanders."

Chloe was in no state of mind to be thinking about last night. That kiss she and Wyatt had shared was still curling her toes, and she wondered what her two sisters would think if they knew she'd been in the enemy's arms.

"Wyatt was…nice at times. Despicable at others. The man just doesn't understand what children need. The only thing he relates to is money and possessions. He thinks all we Murdocks know about is cows and horses and he doesn't want the twins to grow up in such limited surroundings."

"And what does he want the twins to know about?" Justine asked tartly. "The price of raw crude and how much money it takes to drill for it?"

Rose looked at both her sisters. "I think you should both calm down and give Wyatt a chance. He doesn't know us, and we don't know him. Once he sees how things around here really are, he might have a different opinion about where the twins should grow up."

"Oh, Rose," Chloe said with a weary sigh. "You're far too open-minded. I thought you could spot a skunk when you saw one."

"As far as we know, the man hasn't taken any legal action to take the twins away from you. Until then, I'm going to remain hopeful."

"But what if he does file some sort of suit against us? How will we fight it? He's rich. A court battle wouldn't hurt him. We'd have to file bankruptcy. And wouldn't that look good for the Murdock case?''

Just as Rose was making a calming gesture at Chloe, Dr. Bellamy strode into the waiting room. He smiled fondly at the three of them.

"Sorry it took so long, girls, but we've had a busy morning.'' His gaze singled out Justine. "You're looking pert and pretty. Had any more pains?''

Justine shook her head. "No. I'm feeling fine.''

"Good,'' the doctor said with satisfaction, then turned his gaze to include all three women. "Now about Kitty. I've just read the X rays and her ankle has two major fractures and possibly a torn ligament. The orthopedic surgeon can tell more about that once he operates.''

"Operates?'' Chloe repeated worriedly. Dr. Bellamy nodded. "I'm afraid so. Though I'm not certain, I'm pretty sure her ankle will have to be pinned.''

"Oh, dear Aunt Kitty,'' Justine murmured.

"Will it be a serious operation?'' Rose wanted to know.

"Kitty is a very healthy woman. She'll come through this fine, I assure you. But I should warn you the complete recuperation time for her ankle will probably be at least eight weeks, six at the earliest.''

The doctor's prognosis was exactly what Chloe had feared. Yet the problem of being shorthanded on the ranch was a minor thing compared to her aunt's health. Getting Kitty well again was all that really mattered. They would somehow handle the rest.

"We'll make sure she takes care of herself,'' Chloe assured the doctor.

He smiled. "I don't think you're going to have the chance. I've already made arrangements at the hospital in Roswell for Kitty's surgery. She's going to stay there with a friend until she gets back on her feet. As for now, I've given her an injection for pain and a nurse will be wheeling her out in a few minutes. Can some of you drive her over to Roswell later today?''

"Of course, Dr. Bellamy. We'll make sure she gets there," Rose told him.

After the doctor left, Chloe stood and faced her two sisters. "We know Lucille is a good friend of Aunt Kitty's and I'm sure she'd take good care of her, but don't you think she needs to be with her family at a time like this?''

Rose got to her feet and pulled the straps of her purse up on her shoulder. "Aunt Kitty knows you already have your hands full, Chloe. Justine is pregnant, besides having Charlie to care for, and I'm stretched thin helping you with the ranch and seeing after my own home. She'll be much better off recuperating in Roswell where Lucille can see to her needs and she won't feel like a burden to us.''

"Thank goodness one of you has a level head," Kitty spoke up as the nurse wheeled her into the waiting room.

The three women rushed over to their aunt. Chloe kissed her cheek, Rose grabbed her hand and Justine, always the nurse, began to examine her ankle.

"You're going to be all right, Aunt Kitty," Chloe said, sniffing back her tears.

Kitty shook her head as though she couldn't believe her nieces were making such an unnecessary fuss over her. But the smile on her face said she was enjoying it.

"Of course I'm going to be all right! Now get me out of here. I've already called Lucille and told her I'd be there by lunchtime. She's saving me a piece of cheesecake.''

Later that afternoon, Chloe was changing Adam's diaper on the living-room couch when the doorbell rang.

"Just a minute," she called. She hurriedly secured the diaper, then hefting Adam onto her hip, hurried over to the door.

To her dismay she opened it to find Wyatt standing on the porch.

"Hello," he said, amazed at just how much the sight of her affected him. He'd been with her only last night yet a strange exhilaration poured through him as though he'd been yearning for months to see her face and his wish had finally come true. "May I come in?"

Chloe supposed she'd been staring, but she hadn't expected to see him today. Nor had she planned on feeling so mesmerized by the sight of him.

"Uh—yes, of course." She stepped back to allow him entry into the living room. For once in her life, Chloe was acutely aware of her worn jeans and stained work shirt. Her hair was gathered at the back of her head in a messy braid and her face was bare of makeup. Thank goodness she'd just given the twins a bath.

"I know I should have probably called first, but I was...afraid you might try to put me off."

"I doubt anyone has ever been able to put you off," she said. Walking back over to the couch, she took a seat, then sat Adam down on the floor between her legs. A few feet away, Anna was asleep in the playpen.

Seeing she wasn't going to offer him a seat, Wyatt took it upon himself and sat down in an armchair opposite her. "I'm surprised to find you here in the house. Don't you have work to do with your horses?"

For a moment she wondered if he'd heard about Kitty's accident, but she didn't see how. He didn't know anyone in this area.

"Plenty of it. But at the moment I'm taking care of the twins."

He glanced around him. "Your aunt isn't here?"

Chloe grimly shook her head. "Aunt Kitty broke her ankle this morning. It has to be operated on so she's gone to Roswell."

"Oh. I'm sorry to hear that. How did she break it?"

And he honestly looked like he was sorry. The idea that he might actually care about her aunt made Chloe feel a little better. If the man had even an ounce of compassion in him, then she had to believe there was hope he'd finally see the light about the twins and her resolve to be their mother.

"She was walking out behind the house early this morning before daylight and stepped in a hole," Chloe explained. "It was one of those simple accidents that make you want to kick yourself for not paying closer attention."

"How long will she be gone?"

Chloe knew his mind was already at work. She could see the calm, calculating look in his gray eyes.

"Six weeks at least," she said, then waited to hear his suggestion about how perfect a time it would be for Adam and Anna to go to Houston. The mere idea made Chloe want to pull Adam back into her arms and hold him tightly.

"That's obviously going to make things hard on you around here. Is there anyone who can help with the twins?"

She fidgeted with the hem of her shirt. There wasn't any point lying to the man. From his earlier comments, she knew he wasn't going to disappear back to Houston any time soon. He'd be able to see for himself there was no one to take care of the twins but herself.

"Not at the moment. But I'll find someone. Rose and her stepdaughter, Emily, will shoulder some of my load down at the stable."

Even though Chloe had probably said more insulting, infuriating things to him than any male or female ever had, the idea of one more hardship falling on her shoulders didn't necessarily please him.

"I'm sure this was the last thing you needed to have happen," he said, watching Adam wobble to a standing position with the careful aid of Chloe's finger.

She praised the baby boy's accomplishment then kissed him on the cheek before she turned to Wyatt. "I could think of worse things happening."

Like his coming here and announcing he wanted the twins, Wyatt thought, suddenly feeling like an ass but not really knowing why. He had every right, every reason to concern himself with Belinda's children. He had no reason to feel guilty about causing Chloe Murdock extra grief. But he did.

Wyatt got to his feet and rubbed his palms down the thighs of his jeans. "Maybe I should go," he said as it dawned on him that, except for the twins, he and Chloe were alone.

Easing up without breaking Adam's balance, Chloe heard herself say, "Nonsense. You just got here and I was about to make a fresh pot of coffee."

For a moment Wyatt couldn't believe she was inviting him to stay. "You won't dose mine with arsenic, will you?"

Her smile was tentative, but teasing. "Just a little rat poison ought to shut you up for a while."

"That makes me feel a whole lot better."

They walked slowly to the kitchen so that Adam could walk with the help of Chloe's two hands.

The baby squealed with delight at being mobile and Wyatt couldn't help but be touched by the sight of Chloe's gentleness and Adam's total dependence on her.

"I see the babies don't necessarily take naps at the same time," Wyatt said as the three of them entered the kitchen.

"No. They have habits and personalities of their own."

She sat Adam in the extra playpen they kept in the kitchen and gave him a graham cracker to chew on.

As she put the coffee on to brew, Wyatt came to the cabinets and leaned his hip against the counter. From the corner of her eye she noticed he was dressed casually today in a pair of blue jeans and a navy blue shirt checked with small white windowpanes. On his feet were a pair of brown roper boots, a city man's way of dressing "cowboy," she supposed, and smiled to herself.

"Chloe, about last night—"

"I've forgotten about last night." She hadn't, but she definitely needed to make him think so.

He stepped closer, prompting her to look at him. As soon as her eyes met his, heat poured through her body and she could think of nothing but the way it had felt to be held in his arms, to taste his lips.

"I've had a little time to think about those checks you showed me. And..."

He stopped and Chloe wondered what he was thinking as his gray eyes roamed her face. Did he think she'd asked him to stay for coffee because of that kiss last night? No. Surely not. It wasn't in her to play seductress even when she was dressed in her sexiest outfit, much less a grubby shirt and worn jeans. And even if he did think she was sending him provocative signals, the man wasn't wet behind the ears, nor was he subtle. He'd simply come out and tell her she'd be wasting her time to try and change his mind about the twins with feminine wiles.

When he failed to go on, Chloe finally prompted, "And what?"

His eyes flickered away from her face, then back to it. "I want you to know I'm not proud of what my sister has done to your family. I'm not saying she was blackmailing your father for the money. That I don't want to believe. But it's obvious she was either asking your father for money or demanding it. Whatever the case, it was wrong of her."

A few days ago, even last night, Chloe would have taken tremendous satisfaction in hearing him admit his sister had maligned her family. But today it didn't seem all that important. Maybe Rose's ability to forgive was rubbing off on her. Or maybe she was beginning to see that blaming someone else for her troubles wasn't showing the true grit of a Murdock.

"Thank you for saying that, Wyatt. That's the only payment I wanted from you."

Yes, he could see that now. But it was still incredible to him that even though she'd lost her finances, money wasn't the real issue with her. She was more concerned about apologies and the right and wrong of it.

Coffee began to pour into the glass carafe, filling the room with its pungent smell. Glad for something to do, Chloe gathered cups and saucers.

"There's plenty of Aunt Kitty's cherry cobbler left. Would you like some with your coffee?"

"I never turn down dessert. Even if it is the middle of the afternoon," he said.

Chloe filled two small bowls with cobbler and placed them on a tray with the cups. After she poured the coffee, she carried the whole thing over to the kitchen table.

Wyatt took a seat and Chloe checked on Adam in the playpen. The baby had fallen asleep, so she covered him with a thick blanket before she joined Wyatt at the table.

Noticing he was waiting for her to get settled before he ate, she said, "Don't wait on me. You'll find you have to eat whenever you can around here and not worry about manners. Something usually happens and you have to jump up. It might be hours before you get a chance to eat again."

"I was just thinking this is the quietest time I can ever remember spending anywhere," he said, digging into his cobbler.

"I don't think of this place as quiet, but I suppose to someone like you who lives in the fast lane it's as slow as Christmas turkey."

"Is that slow?"

She gave him an impish little smile. "It takes all year to get it. I'd say that's pretty slow."

"I didn't realize you thought I lived in the fast lane," he replied. "Do I look like a party goer?"

She frowned as she slipped a bite of cobbler into her mouth. "No, you look like a man who works a lot."

His lips twisted. "You couldn't know that about me."

From the corner of her eye, Chloe watched his fingers curl around his coffee cup. They were long, strong fingers, the skin tanned and sprinkled with dark hair. He wore no rings or jewelry of any sort. Not because he couldn't afford it, obviously. He wasn't a flashy man. In fact, she found him very unpretentious.

"Let's just say I have a hunch that you get up with work on your mind and go to bed with work on your mind. You don't eat breakfast and grab anything you can for lunch because you either have meetings or phone calls to make. You take work home with you and rarely have friends over. You go out on occasion, but only after you've taken the time to choose your date carefully. And even then, you're usually wondering if you'll ever meet a woman who has any depth to her. Am I anywhere close?"

Last night Chloe had correctly perceived his thinking, and now she'd pretty well summed up his life. Could the woman see inside him or something?

He shifted uncomfortably on the padded chair. If she knew all that about him, maybe she could see he was, in spite of a gallant fight, growing attracted to her.

"You're..." He frowned, then with a conceding shrug of his shoulder, chuckled lowly. "How did you know?"

She laughed and it felt, oh, so good. "I have friends who've moved to the city. And I've spent a lot of time in Santa Fe. It's a western city, but it moves fast."

He took another bite of cobbler and wondered how long it had been since he'd sat eating like this and not have his mind on acquiring a new drilling company, or flying to Dallas or Tulsa or New Orleans. His thoughts were normally on mergers or buy outs, of what the overseas sales of raw crude were doing and how it was going to affect his own market.

But with Chloe, all of that seemed to fade away to another place and time. When he looked at her, his priorities became fuzzy and jumbled.

On the way out here today, Wyatt had told himself he was coming to see the twins and to attempt to change Chloe's mind about their future. After all, he'd already been away from his office in Houston far longer than he'd first anticipated. He didn't have time to simply wait around until she finally realized he would be the best thing for the twins. He needed to nudge her thinking along. But he had to admit all of that was only part of why he'd driven the twenty-mile trip. He couldn't quit thinking about the kiss they'd exchanged last night. Even now, the memory of it sent slivers of heat curling around in his stomach and an incredible urge deep inside him to do it all over again.

"You don't exactly move at a slow pace around here," he countered, remembering the first day he'd seen her exercising the horses. She'd buzzed around the stable like a worker bee with a death sentence. "And I doubt you really have friends over very often, or go out on a date more than once every two months. And when you do, he either bores you or irritates the hell out of you. Am I anywhere close?"

"You make it sound like my life isn't that much different from yours. But you know it is," she told him.

"Just tell me if I'm right or not," he persisted.

She watched her finger make a slow circle around the rim of her coffee cup. "You're right about some of it."

"The dating part?"

Her eyes lifted from the cup to his face. "Why do you want to know about that?"

Wyatt shrugged and tried to appear casual. "Well, you insist you want to be the twins' mother. It makes me wonder why you wouldn't want to marry and give them a father."

Of course she should have known it was the twins he was interested in. Not her. "We've already been over this issue before. If—and this is a remote if—I ever found a man I thought would be good for me and the twins, I wouldn't hesitate to marry. But I don't ever expect to find him.''

Unsettled by his question and the probe of his gray eyes, Chloe got up from the table and carried her empty bowl to the sink. Kitty's accident this morning had left things undone in the kitchen. Dirty dishes were still waiting to be washed and the floor was gritty.

She fit the stopper in the sink and turned on the hot water. Wyatt might as well learn she didn't have time to sit and socialize with him or anyone.

I don't ever expect to find him. Chloe's words rolled slowly over and over in Wyatt's mind as he watched her from his seat at the table. She was hiding something. Sooner or later he was going to find out what it was. And then maybe he would understand what drove her to work herself to the point of exhaustion during the day, then spend her nights with two babies who weren't really hers.

Before he could stop himself, Wyatt went over to where she stood with her hands plunged in the soapy water. He dropped his empty cup and bowl in with the mound she was working on.

''Chloe,'' he began, ''I know I'm an outsider. And I don't know about all the things you have to do around here to keep the ranch going. But I do know you can't manage alone. Now that your aunt is out of commission for a while, you—''

She whirled on him and the absolute terror he saw in her eyes halted the rest of his words.

''I know what you're going to say. Now is the time for you to take the twins, right?''

A few days ago he probably would have said just that. But today the idea hadn't as yet crossed his mind. He'd been too busy worrying about Chloe and wondering what he could do to ease her burden. Where, along the way had his thinking changed? Why did his heart soften every time he looked at her? This wasn't the way he'd planned for things to go.

The horrible whiteness of her face tore at him and before he could analyze his actions, he reached out and touched her arm. She immediately flinched, but didn't pull away as she continued to hold his gaze in the grip of hers.

"No. That wasn't what I was going to say at all."

Confusion flickered in her eyes and her lips parted with surprise. It was all Wyatt could do not to pull her into his arms and taste those soft pink lips once again.

"Then what—"

"I was going to offer myself to fill in for Kitty," he said quickly before he had time to ask himself if he'd gone mad.

Chapter Seven

Chloe laughed. Softly at first, then louder. Wyatt was bewildered by the response. He'd expected a tirade of cursing or some sort of sarcastic rejection. Yet she continued to laugh until there were tears in her eyes and on her cheeks.

"Chloe. Chloe," he said gently and pulled her into his arms. She didn't try to resist him, but her body was stiff and rigid as he smoothed a hand down her back. "Why are you crying?"

"I—I'm not. I'm laughing." She hiccuped and scrubbed her eyes with her fists.

"You are crying, and there's no need for it," he assured her.

Like a moth testing a flame, she leaned her cheek against his chest, drew it back, then finally decided to settle it against the beat of his heart.

"Why not?" she asked in a wobbly voice. "The idea of an oilman becoming a cook and baby-sitter is enough to make anyone cry."

He smiled over her head. "I don't think the world will run out of gasoline if I lay off work a few more days."

"That wasn't what I meant!" Her composure gathered, she started to pull away from him. Wyatt's hand caught the back of her head and she found her face a breath away from his.

"What do you think about the idea?"

She couldn't believe he'd offered, or how much it touched her that he had. "I think you're crazy. You can't stay here with me!"

Wyatt hadn't exactly thought about staying here at nights, but now that she'd brought it up, he knew he wouldn't be much help unless he was here on the ranch twenty-four hours a day.

"Why not?" he asked.

She wished he'd let her go. She couldn't think sensibly while he was touching her, while the male scent of him swirled in her head and his tempting lips were only a breath away.

"Because. We'd be alone."

"The twins will be with us," he reasoned.

She groaned. "Two ten-month-old babies can't be considered chaperones."

One of his brows arched. "You think we need chaperones?"

She drew in a sharp little breath. "After last night, I know we do."

Last night. Yeah, last night was still on his mind and Wyatt just had to see if it was still on hers.

Lowering his head just a fraction, he covered her lips with his and drew her into the tight circle of his arms.

Chloe told herself she wanted to pull away from him. She even put her palms against his chest to pry some distance between them, but that was as far as her resistance took her. Heat and a sexual excitement she had long ago forgotten swept through her body and insisted that her lips cling hungrily to his, that her arms move up his chest and around his neck.

"Chloe," he murmured as his mouth lifted to trail hot moist kisses behind her ear, down her neck and across the tender line of her jaw.

Her hands gripped the top of his shoulders as her head reeled with sudden longing. She wanted this man! How could that be? He could only hurt her. Yet every fiber of her body longed for his mouth, his touch, his love.

The shocking direction of her thoughts gave her the strength to twist out of his arms and back away. "This is exactly why you can't stay here!"

Her breasts were heaving and color burned high on her cheeks. She was the most beautiful woman he'd ever seen and at the moment all he wanted was to crush her mouth beneath his, kiss her until she was soft and pliant in his arms and her green eyes glowed with dark desire.

"You can't say you didn't enjoy that," he said, his voice faintly accusing.

"I…" Her eyes dropped to the dusty floor and her teeth pressed into her bottom lip. "I liked it all right. That's what makes it so bad."

His brows drew together. "Bad? You call that bad?"

Her jaw dropped. "Have you not heard anything I've been saying to you these past few days? I don't go playing around with men! Or does that not mean anything to you?"

He was still shaking from the encounter and she wanted to label it as play! He'd never known such an exasperating woman. "You think what just happened between us was playing around?"

She turned her back to him. "By any name it shouldn't have happened."

He eyed the stiff, rigid line of her back and shoulders. "Because of who I am?"

"That's part of it."

And what was the other part? Wyatt desperately wanted to ask her. But he instinctively knew now wasn't the time to press her about her love life. Besides, that was something he was going to have to forget entirely.

"Chloe, forget the past five minutes. What just happened won't happen again." At least he'd try like hell not to let it happen again, he told himself. "I didn't offer to help you with the twins just as a means to get to your body."

Slowly she turned around and eyed him skeptically. "It sure felt that way a few moments ago."

Frustrated, he raked a hand through his hair. For some reason, Wyatt felt his getting custody of the twins hinged on whether Chloe allowed him to stay here on the Bar M for the next few weeks. Not under any circumstances could he let her know just how attracted he was to her. Otherwise, her boot was going to be kicking his rear right out the front door.

"That was—totally out of character for me," he explained. "Just a sudden urge that I—acted upon."

"And how do I know you won't have another sudden urge?"

"Chloe—" He took a step toward her and she held up a hand to deter him from getting any closer.

"Wyatt, I have enough problems already. The last thing I need is to let you seduce me into making love to you."

Just hearing her say those words sent a surge of desire through him, but he did his best to ignore it. "I won't. It won't be that way."

She said nothing, just folded her arms across her breast.

He went on, "Look, Chloe, I'm not crazy. You're the last woman on earth I need to become involved with. Just give me the chance to let me help you. Besides, the twins are the real issue here. Not me, or you, or us."

That was certainly true enough, Chloe thought. And she wasn't vain enough to think Wyatt was really interested in her as a woman. She was far more worried about the reckless impulses she felt everytime the man touched her. But if he kept his distance as he said he would, then it might be an altogether good thing to let him see exactly what he'd be getting into with the twins.

"You're right. The twins are the issue."

"Then you're going to accept my offer?"

Was she crazy? Or just desperate enough to say yes?

Before Chloe could weigh the answer to those questions, the telephone rang.

Glad for the interruption, Chloe walked to the end of the cabinets and pulled the receiver down from the wall phone. As soon as she answered, Justine's voice came back at her.

"Chloe, I've got some news for you."

"Oh, about Aunt Kitty? Surely she hasn't already had her surgery? It's only been a few hours since Rose took her to Roswell."

"No. Rose assured me she was going to stay there until Kitty was safely out of surgery and I haven't heard from her yet. Have you?"

"No."

"Oh. Well, I called to let you know Roy checked out your Mr. Sanders."

Chloe's eyes flew guiltily over to Wyatt, who had begun to wash the dishes she'd started on a few minutes ago.

"And—what did he have to say?" she asked trying her best to sound casual.

"Just what you thought. From what Roy says, the man is Mr. Good Guy. Not even an old parking ticket."

She felt glad and torn and guilty all at once. "Well, that's…well, at least we don't have to wonder anymore."

There was a pause, then Justine said, "Chloe, you sound a little strange. Are you feeling all right? You're not worrying yourself sick over Aunt Kitty, are you? I promise the surgery will be a snap for her. She and Lucille will be playing cards by tomorrow.''

"I'm...not worrying about Aunt Kitty. I—I've just been trying to figure out what to do about keeping up the horses and the stable. Rose and Emily can't do it all.''

"Roy is going to try to make it by there this evening and help with whatever he can.''

Chloe continued to watch Wyatt as he washed dish after dish and stacked them on a nearby drainboard. She'd never seen a man at work in this kitchen. And for that man to be Wyatt made it an even stranger sight.

"Thank Roy for the offer,'' Chloe said with sudden decision, "but I'll be able to handle things myself.''

"But the twins—'' Justine began to argue only to have Chloe interrupt, "Will be taken care of. I've already got someone for the job.''

"Job? Chloe! What are you talking about? I know you're in a desperate spot right now. But we can't afford to hire anyone!''

"This person doesn't require pay.''

There was another long pause and then Justine sucked in an audible breath. "Oh, my Lord, you're not talking about Wyatt Sanders, are you?''

"I am.''

"Chloe, what are you thinking? What has he done to you?''

Justine's choice of words brought a blush to Chloe's cheeks. "Nothing. I know what I'm doing. I'll explain it all later.''

She hung up before Justine could say more, then walked slowly over to where Wyatt was still working at the sink. As she propped her hip against the counter, he turned his head sideways to look at her.

"That was my sister, Justine,'' she explained, her heart thumping as though she was on the verge of taking a dangerous high dive.

"She's heard from your aunt?"

Chloe shook her head and knew her expression was sheepish. "She called to let me know Roy had run a check on you."

He didn't reply, and Chloe said, "I won't blame you if you're angry. But it wasn't the sort of thing I wanted to keep from you."

If anything, Wyatt respected her for her honesty. "I suppose it should make me mad to think you people distrusted me so much that you felt you had to go behind my back and dig into my life. But..." He paused and shrugged. "I'm not angry. If I were in your place I would've probably done the same thing."

Chloe didn't know why she was so relieved. It shouldn't matter whether his feelings were bruised. But it did. She didn't want to hurt Wyatt for any reason. When and how she'd come to that conclusion, she didn't know, but it was there in her heart just the same.

"I'm glad you see it that way." She rubbed at a scarred spot on the countertop. "I—uh, told my sister you were going to help me with the twins."

He plopped the last saucer onto the drainboard and reached for a tea towel. Drying his hands, he smiled and said, "You won't regret it, Chloe."

She probably would, but it was too late to worry about that now. Straightening away from the cabinet, she said, "Well, I've decided this would be a good opportunity to find out just how badly you want to be the twins' father."

It was all Wyatt could do not to yelp with joy and smack a kiss on her lips. The woman was finally giving in. If things kept going like this, he might be able to get the twins out of this place sooner than he thought.

"I'll drive into Ruidoso right now and pack up my things at the motel. I should be able to make it back in an hour and a half at the latest," he told her, glancing at his watch.

"You're starting today?"

Seeing the surprise on her face, Wyatt said, "Why not? You have horses to care for. You can't do that and watch two babies at the same time."

"I haven't forgotten you don't know anything about babies. Have you?"

He gave her a lazy smile, and Chloe's heart thumped with foolish anticipation.

"I haven't been around babies before," he agreed. "But I don't know anything about caring for horses either. And from where I'm standing, the babies seem to be the far safer of the two jobs."

Chloe couldn't help but laugh. "You may want to reevaluate that opinion after a couple of days."

He tossed the tea towel on the cabinet counter and rubbed his palms together in a gesture of readiness. "How hard could the job be? Two babies and a little cooking. It'll be a vacation compared to the hours I put in with the oil company."

Smiling to herself, she said, "Good. I'm sure a vacation like this is just what you need."

"Chloe, I realize I told Justine I couldn't find any sort of criminal past on Wyatt Sanders," Roy said as Chloe poured a measurable amount of oats into a black rubber feed bucket. "But that didn't mean it was okay for you to turn the twins and the house over to him."

She waved her hand at her brother-in-law who'd just gotten off work and was still wearing his sheriff's uniform.

"Justine said you called him Mr. Good Guy."

He gave an exasperated snort. "Of course I'd say that to her. She's going to have our baby in the next few weeks. I don't want her worrying about anything."

Chloe walked over to a room where the feed was stored and tossed the half-empty sack of oats against the wall.

Turning back to Roy, she said, "Then you don't think the man can be trusted?"

He lifted his Stetson and ran a hand through his hair. "I didn't say that, Chloe. I don't know the man. I'm not in any position to give you an opinion one way or the other. I just wonder if you know what you're doing."

Chloe sighed. "You're worried the man is going to be staying in the house—with the twins."

"And with you," he added.

Roy's concern touched her. He and Harlan were both like brothers. She valued their opinions and, even more, their love. Yet she was as certain as the day was long that she had nothing to fear from Wyatt. At least not physically. Emotionally was an altogether different matter.

"I know how to take care of myself, Roy. And believe me, I wouldn't let anyone around the twins if I didn't trust them. You know that."

From another sack, she poured sweet feed into the bucket of oats, then mixed the whole lot with her hands.

Roy stood silently contemplating her for a moment. Of Justine and her two sisters, Chloe was the hardest one to figure. Even though she was outwardly emotional at times, Roy didn't believe she ever let anyone see the real her, the one she hid behind the tough skin she presented to the world.

"All right, Chloe. I trust your judgment. I won't bring up the matter again. Now," he went on, glancing around the stable. "What do you need me to do?"

She waved him toward the door. "Not a thing. I've gotten nearly all the horses fed and watered. I still have to give Martin his bottle, but the way he eats, that doesn't take long. Whatever is left to do, Rose will help me with tomorrow."

She started to heft the feed bucket off the ground, but Roy quickly grabbed it. With an appreciative smile, she pointed to where a black filly was impatiently pawing the stall door.

After he'd hung the bucket for the horse to eat, Chloe said, "Thanks, Roy. Now if you really want to do me a favor, why don't you stop by the house and say hello to Wyatt? When I left him a couple of hours ago, one twin was asleep and the other one was yelling for food. He might need a little male encouragement."

Roy grinned and gave her a little salute from the brim of his hat. "I'll do that. And call me if you need me."

It was well after dark when Chloe walked back to the house. The moment she entered the kitchen, the smell of scorched food filled her nostrils.

Wyatt was nowhere in sight. She went to check the pots on the cookstove. In the largest one, she found spaghetti boiled dry and sizzling on the bottom of the pan. On the next burner was a pot of tomato sauce. Thank goodness, it still had enough liquid to simmer.

She walked out to the living room, then down the hall toward the nursery. "Wyatt?"

"In here, Chloe." His answer was immediately followed by a loud, angry yell from Adam.

Reaching the doorway of the nursery, she saw Wyatt bending over the crib trying to catch Anna, who was crawling around the bed with only half of her diaper fastened. Adam was standing up at the railing, his face beet red as he squalled at the top of his lungs.

"Having a little trouble?" she asked with calm sweetness.

He shot her a frustrated look. "Why won't she lie still until I get her diaper on? And he," Wyatt said, turning an irritated scowl on Adam, "has no reason to be crying. He just drained a whole bottle a few minutes ago."

Chloe stepped into the room. "Babies do cry for reasons

other than hunger. He probably doesn't like the way you and his sister are jostling him around.''

"Well, I can't put him on the floor. He'll run off. I've already tried it. That's when Anna decided she wanted to crawl instead of get dressed."

Deciding to take a little pity on him, she stepped up to the crib. "See if you can pacify Adam and I'll finish Anna's diaper."

He lifted Adam out of the crib, and the two of them left the room. Chloe couldn't help but notice the boy hushed as soon as he was in Wyatt's arms.

After she'd finished with Anna's floppy diaper, she carried the little girl into the kitchen. Wyatt was over at the cookstove trying to balance Adam on his hip with one hand and stir spaghetti sauce with the other.

"The pasta is ruined," he announced with disgust.

"I know. I already looked."

"I suppose this never happens to Kitty."

His tone dared her to make fun of him. Chloe was careful to keep a straight face. "Not too often. But she does have her rough moments."

"And you? I suppose you could have handled this with one arm tied behind your back?"

It was obvious to Chloe he was a man who liked to excel at everything he did. Smiling wanly, she walked over to him. "Not really," she admitted with a shake of her head. "And there's no need for you to beat yourself up over a pot of scorched pasta. I don't expect you to be perfect at this job."

He cocked a brow at her. "Who said anything about trying to be perfect?"

Adam found Wyatt's ear and jerked it. Chloe couldn't help but laugh as he tried to dodge the baby's rough affection.

"All men like to think they're perfect. I'm sure you're no exception."

"I don't have an ego that has to be fed, Chloe."

She gave him a perky smile. "Good. Because right now I'm more concerned about feeding our stomachs."

After settling Anna in the playpen, she went to the cabinets and rummaged through the food items. Wyatt stood to one side, his eyes taking in the provocative curves of her body as she stood on tiptoe and reached to push the canned and boxed goods from side to side.

"There's no more pasta, if that's what you're looking for," he said after a moment.

"Here's a bag of macaroni. That will do." She tossed it onto the countertop.

"Macaroni won't taste as good," he told her.

"Who's picky? I'll eat anything," Chloe assured him.

Wyatt wasn't picky. He could eat anything, too. But he knew she'd been working hard and he'd wanted to have something decent ready for her to eat.

"Okay, I'll cook the macaroni."

She reached for Adam. "Here, let me put him in the playpen with his sister. You can't cook with a baby on your hip."

"He'll start bawling again," Wyatt warned.

"I doubt it. But if he does, let him. It won't hurt him to cry for a few minutes. Otherwise, he's going to have you hornswoggled into carrying him around all day long."

"I've been at this four hours, and you already think I'm spoiling him?"

Chloe literally pulled the child from Wyatt's grasp. "Wyatt, will you relax? I'm not thinking any such thing. I'm just trying to give you a little advice." She put Adam down in the playpen, then walked back over to Wyatt who was standing, his arms folded across his chest as though he was ready and waiting for more of her so-called advice.

"Look, Wyatt, I never gripe about free help. I want you to realize how much I appreciate it. I don't care what you burn or how much you spoil the babies."

He visibly relaxed. "I guess I have been a little on the defensive, haven't I?"

When she nodded, he chuckled. "I just didn't want to make a mess of things right off the bat."

Chloe laughed. "The only real mess I see around here is me," she said, glancing down at her dirty clothes. "So if you can manage a few minutes without me, I'm going to go wash up."

She left the room and Wyatt got busy putting water on to boil for the macaroni. As he scraped the burned pasta into the garbage pail, he could only wonder what was making him act like such an idiot. He knew Chloe didn't expect him to be the perfect daddy to the twins or some great chef here in the kitchen. Yet he wanted to be those things for her. He wanted her to see him as a man who wasn't just successful in the oil business, but a man whom she could count on for anything. Was this his ego talking, or his heart? Either way he knew he had to forget about pleasing Chloe. He wasn't here for her sake. He was here for the twins and nothing else.

When Chloe returned to the kitchen several minutes later, the twins were playing quietly in their playpen, the macaroni was cooked and smothered in spicy tomato sauce. A tossed salad was on the table and Wyatt was taking garlic bread out of the oven.

"Mmm, that smells delicious. What can I do to help?"

He looked around to see she'd showered and changed into a short-sleeved copper colored sweater and a pair of matching corduroy pants. Except for a few loose strands, her hair was caught loosely atop her head with a tortoise-shell clamp. Wyatt had never known a woman who could look so good without even trying.

"I think everything is ready, except icing the glasses for tea. Or would you rather drink wine with dinner?"

Drink wine alone with him? Not on her life. She needed

to be wide awake and keep all her senses in a straight line. "No, thanks. Tea will be fine for me."

While he placed the rest of the food on the table, she prepared their drinks.

"Which twin do you want to feed?" she asked while dragging two high chairs from the corner of the room.

Wyatt had never fed himself and a baby at the same time. He figured the task would be a little bit like rubbing his head and patting his belly at the same time. But if Chloe could do it, he at least had to try.

"I'll take Adam. He's more used to me than Anna. Besides, he's been trying his best to give me a bad case of indigestion all evening. Now it's my turn to give him one."

Wyatt joined her at the table and helped her position the high chairs next to both their chairs. "What are the babies going to eat?" he asked. "Some more of that gooey stuff I gave them this afternoon?"

She laughed at his description of pureed carrots and spinach. "No. We'll chop up the macaroni for them. They love the stuff."

There had been times in the past when Wyatt had taken dates out for dinner at elegant restaurants where there was candlelight and lots of fresh flowers. The women had always been wearing tasteful designer clothes, their nails had been perfectly manicured and their hair groomed in the latest fashion.

But those restaurants couldn't compare to the relaxed hominess of this warm kitchen. Those women had never looked as appealing or beautiful as Chloe did as she sat feeding Anna and herself the macaroni he'd cooked. And he realized if Sandra could hear and see him now, she'd think he'd gone crazy. A few days ago he would have thought it himself. But a few days ago he hadn't known Chloe or the babies. He hadn't known being with a woman could be so simple and yet so good.

"There was so much commotion when you first came in, I forgot to tell you your sister Rose called. She said Kitty's surgery was over. Everything went fine and she would see you tomorrow."

"Oh, that is good news. Did she say how long Aunt Kitty would have to stay in the hospital?"

"She's getting out tomorrow afternoon."

Relief washed over Chloe. "I'll call her tomorrow night. I'm sure she'll be wanting to know how things are going here."

Wyatt offered Adam a spoonful of macaroni. The baby wrinkled his nose and stared at the food as if it were an offending object.

"See," Wyatt said to Chloe, "the little monster is deliberately defying me."

"Eat it yourself."

"What?"

Chloe laughed at the confused look on his face. "I said, eat the macaroni yourself. He'll decide he wants some in a minute."

Wyatt followed her advice and swallowed the spoonful of food. Adam regarded this as hilarious and started giggling out loud. Anna soon imitated her brother and in the process spewed tomato sauce and bits of macaroni down the front of her face and bib.

Groaning, Chloe grabbed a napkin and attempted to clean Anna's face. Wyatt threw up his hands and shook his head.

"This has to be your best parenting instruction yet," he told her, chuckling.

"I can't help it if the twins think you look funny. Most of the time it's monkey see, monkey do. You eat it and they want to eat it."

"Well, this time it backfired."

So it did, Chloe thought, but at least Wyatt had loosened up. Maybe before this was all over he would come to see that perfection wasn't what the twins needed. Or Houston and his wealth. They needed affection and attention and love. In the next few days she had to make Wyatt see that she could give the twins the things that counted most.

Chapter Eight

When it came time for dessert, which was the last of Kitty's cherry cobbler, the two of them carried it into the living room and ate while the babies played with a stack of colorful plastic blocks Chloe had piled in the middle of the floor for them.

"I could build a fire if you think the room is too cool for the twins," Wyatt offered, remembering the fire she'd had burning last night. It had made the room warm and cozy. And living in Houston he rarely got to enjoy the sight of a burning fireplace.

Chloe shook her head. "It's not as cool tonight, and I don't want to waste the firewood."

For a moment Wyatt considered telling her not to worry about the wood—he'd buy all the firewood she needed. But he didn't. From past experience he knew where that would lead. No sooner than he bought the wood, she'd be needing something else. She'd insist she didn't want him spending his money on her, but in the next breath he'd be hearing the old empty cupboard sob story.

Wyatt wasn't stingy or greedy. In fact, he gave large

sums of money to different charities throughout the year. But being rich had made him a target. And more often than not, he'd had to learn the hard way that people weren't really interested in him, but only what he and his money could do for them.

Maybe Chloe would never be that way. But she was hurting for funds. She might be sorely tempted to use him, and he couldn't let himself give her that chance.

"Where do you buy your firewood? In Ruidoso?"

An odd look crossed her face. "Buy it? I don't buy it, I take the chain saw and the four-wheel drive up the mountain and cut it myself."

Wyatt was so taken aback by her answer he could only stare at her.

Finally, she wiped a finger at the corner of her mouth. "What's the matter? Do I have something on my face?"

No, he did and it was usually called egg. Thank God, she couldn't know what he'd just been thinking. "No—uh—I'm sorry if I was staring. I was just..." He got up and went over to the fireplace and stacked several logs on the cold grate. "Well, just don't worry about the firewood," he said gruffly. "I'll help you cut it."

He wouldn't be here long enough for that, Chloe thought, but she didn't say anything as she watched him stick a match to the kindling. She certainly didn't want Wyatt thinking she was so miserly she sat around in a cold house.

Before long, flames were licking at the logs, radiating heat out over the sitting area. Wyatt stood to one side of the hearth, listening to the snap of the pine and the baby talk the twins were swapping with each other. There were no honking horns or squealing tires, no sirens or shouts from noisy neighbors.

Out here, the only sounds to be heard were the wind whispering through the pines, the occasional nicker of a horse and once, before Chloe had come in from the stable, he thought he'd heard the distant howl of a coyote or wolf. Altogether it was a lonely but peaceful silence and nothing like he'd ever experienced before.

"What do you normally do in the evenings like this?" he asked Chloe.

She was curled up on one end of the sofa, her head resting against the back. At first glance her beauty was the thing he noticed, but on closer inspection he recognized the paleness of her face, the shadows of exhaustion under her eyes.

She should be living in a gentle, tropical climate where she wouldn't have to work in the bitter cold or dry, blistering heat, Wyatt thought. Did she never long for an easier life?

"Rest," she said. Then realizing how that must sound to him, she added, "Sometimes my sisters and their families come over. We eat and play cards and visit. And other times, after the twins are asleep, Aunt Kitty and I watch a movie on the VCR or read." She didn't go on to tell him that most evenings there was laundry to be folded and put away, the kitchen to be cleaned and the babies to be bathed and put to bed.

She instinctively knew that Wyatt had come from a family where there had always been housekeepers to do such manual chores. The women he knew could probably sit around the house in their "good" clothes, read fashion magazines and eat bonbons. Chloe wouldn't mind having a little extra help now and then. But she didn't want a life of leisure.

Wyatt glanced at the television set in the corner of the room. During the times he'd been out here to the ranch, he had yet to see it on. "You don't watch TV?"

She shrugged. "The news and weather. It's hard to keep up with a story while the twins are awake. The first thing you know you're chasing one of them or changing a diaper and," she smiled wanly, "you've missed part of the plot."

Somehow he knew that didn't bother Chloe. She was a woman who obviously put entertainment as the least important of her needs.

Sighing, he stepped off the hearth and walked over to the long paned windows that overlooked the front yard. In the daylight a high mountain range could be seen rising to the north, but tonight it was so dark even the pines shading the yard couldn't be discerned.

From the couch, Chloe watched Wyatt staring out the windows. She knew he was restless. This isolated place, as he'd called it, was probably boring him silly. But Chloe hardly knew what to do about it. She wasn't forcing him to stay. If he wanted to leave, all he had to do was get his things and go.

"It looks very cloudy out tonight. Is it possible for it to snow around here at this time of the year?"

"It's mid-September. In the higher elevations like here on the ranch, anything is possible. We have had a snow flurry in August before."

He smiled and shook his head in disbelief. "We're in the middle of hurricane season at home and it's still as hot as a firecracker."

He moved away from the windows and went over to the twins. Squatting down on his bootheels, he murmured something to the babies, then stacked the scattered blocks in a pyramid between their chubby little legs. The minute he finished, Adam took one healthy swat at the structure and sent the whole lot tumbling down.

Upset by her brother's rowdy attitude, Anna began to pucker up and cry. Wyatt lifted the little girl from the floor and cuddled her in his arms.

"I know, sweetheart," he crooned to her. "Your brother is an ornery little thing. When he gets older we're going to have to teach him some manners."

Anna bellowed louder and pointed her arm at her

brother, who was happily banging the plastic blocks against the tile floor.

Wyatt carried Anna over to a swivel rocker and sat down with her. "Here," he told the baby, "I've got something you can play with."

Chloe watched him fish in the front pocket of his jeans. After a moment he pulled out a beautiful pocket watch on a chain. He swung it temptingly in front of Anna, then allowed her tiny fist to grab it. Naturally, the little girl took the timepiece straight to her mouth.

"Wyatt! She'll ruin your watch," Chloe exclaimed.

"It won't hurt her, will it?"

"No. But she'll get it wet."

"It's waterproof. Besides, if it stops running I can always buy another one and let the twins have this one for a toy."

Chloe groaned inwardly. The twins would be rotten once he left here, she thought, and then her mind froze with dawning reality. How could she have forgotten, even for a moment, that Wyatt planned to take the twins back to Houston with him? Because just for a moment she'd imagined the four of them as a family. She and Wyatt taking care of the twins together. Always. What was the matter with her? Had she gone crazy?

Tell Wyatt how it really is with you. Justine's suggestion crept into Chloe's mind like an insidious snake looking for a crack to wiggle through. What would he really think if she told him she was unable to bear children? Chloe asked herself, then silently cursed as she imagined his response.

He'd pity her, no doubt. Like Richard, he'd probably even go on to tell her what a shame and what an unfair thing to have happened to her. But in the end, he'd say her condition had nothing to do with the twins' future security. Wealth and their chance to have it meant far more to Wyatt than Chloe being childless for the rest of her life.

And maybe he was right, she thought glumly. Maybe she was the one being selfish and narrow minded.

"Chloe? What's the matter?"

She looked at him blankly and he said, "You've got a horrible frown on your face. Do you have a headache?"

As far as she was concerned Wyatt wasn't just a headache, he was a full-blown migraine, the kind that hung on for days. "No. I was just...thinking about something." She got to her feet before he could press her. "I'm going to go clean up the kitchen. Think you can handle the twins for a few minutes?"

She was too tired to be doing the dishes, but he bit down on the words. What was the use of pointing out something she already knew? Especially if he wasn't going to do anything to change her plight? The questions made him so uncomfortable he actually shifted in the chair.

"Why don't you let me clean the kitchen and you watch the twins?" he suggested.

Chloe shook her head and smiled. "You've got Anna pacified and Adam seems to be behaving himself for the moment. Let's not rock the boat. When I finish in the kitchen, I'll come back and get them ready for bed."

A half hour later both twins were sound asleep. Wyatt laid them side by side in the playpen, then covered them with a soft blanket.

In the kitchen he found Chloe dust mopping the floor. The dishes were done, the countertops and cook range cleaned. She'd obviously been busy since she'd left him in the living room.

"Where are the twins?" she asked when she looked up and saw him walking toward her.

"Both asleep. In the playpen." He let out an audible breath. "It's like two little tornadoes have shut down."

Leaning on the mop handle, she smiled at him. "I guess for a person who's never been around babies before, you had a double shock treatment today."

He grinned. "I never stopped to consider how totally dependent babies are. You can't turn your back or leave them alone for one minute."

"That's true."

He glanced toward the cabinet and the coffeemaker. "Would you mind if I made another pot of coffee? I'll clean up the mess."

"Of course I don't mind," she said as she went back to her sweeping. "I want you to make yourself at home here."

She went back to her mopping, and Wyatt began to gather the coffee fixings. While he worked Chloe's comment lingered with him. *Make yourself at home.* It was funny how different that word felt to him now. During the years he'd been growing up, home had been a mammoth two-story house in the old, moneyed section of Houston. Wyatt had grown up having most anything he wanted. The best clothes and a roomful of anything a young boy might want to entertain himself. He'd been in Little League, Scouting and summer camps. Then later he'd advanced to motorcycles, cars, girls and college.

His father had provided him with the best of everything and along the way instilled in him a hard-driving ambition that had gotten him where he was today.

But as far as the Sanders mansion feeling like home, he couldn't say. At the time he'd called it home and he'd known it was a place he could always come back to if need be. Yet it had never felt like this place. There hadn't been babies or messes or laughter or eating in the kitchen. There hadn't been a woman around to nurture or love him. The way Chloe loved the twins.

Glancing over his shoulder, he saw Chloe returning the dust mop to the pantry. "You will join me for a cup, won't you? Or does the caffeine keep you awake?"

She could have told him he was far more potent than caffeine.

"It doesn't make any difference if I drink coffee or not. I...don't sleep very well." And she expected she was going to sleep even less now that he was in the house. How could she close her eyes and go to sleep when she knew he was in bed across the hall from her and that the two of them were alone?

"What time do you get up in the mornings?" he asked.

"Four-thirty. But that doesn't mean you have to. The twins usually don't wake until six or so."

Seeing the coffee had finished dripping, he poured two cups and carried them over to the table. Chloe followed and took a seat kitty-corner from him.

"Maybe you'd better go over your schedule with me," Wyatt suggested. "Otherwise, I'm going to be totally lost."

"There's not that much of a schedule around here," she told him. "I get up, get dressed and go to the stable to feed, then come back and eat breakfast. Afterwards, I go back to the stable to start exercising. Since I have ten horses at the present, I get half of them galloped by lunchtime, the other half by mid-afternoon. Then later in the evening, before it's time to start feeding again, I muck out the dirtiest of the stalls."

"When do you ever have time to do anything else?" he asked, amazed at her daily ritual.

She shrugged and sipped her coffee. "I have to let things go undone. Or Rose and Emily take over for me."

Coffee glistened on her pink lips and without warning, he was thinking of this morning when he'd kissed her. And she'd kissed him back. The taste of her was still with him, niggling at him, reminding him how good it would be to simply touch her hand, if nothing else. He'd never in his life felt such a physical longing for anyone and the fact left him feeling strangely vulnerable.

"If you do all you say you do, what is there left around the place for Rose to do?"

She laughed softly. "I know to someone who isn't familiar with ranch work it seems like things move slowly and there couldn't be much to do other than watch the cows graze in the pasture, but believe me, there is. After Daddy died, Rose and I split the work accordingly between us. She'd always worked with the cows and me the horses so we kept things that way. She has several hundred head of cattle to keep up with over several thousand acres of land. During the winter, feed and hay have to be hauled for miles across rough pastureland. She has to ride fenceline. And on a spread this large, that means hundreds of miles of it. The windmills also have to be checked periodically and there're always sick animals to be doctored, heifers needing help calving. The list goes on and on. It's a never-ending job."

Absently tracing the handle of the coffee mug with his fingertip, Wyatt contemplated all that she'd just told him. This place, Chloe's life, and that of her family, were so very different from what he'd expected. When he first got to New Mexico, he'd figured he was going to find three high-rolling women who blamed his sister for the ranch's decline, rather than the rock-bottom cattle prices of the past several months.

But now, after viewing the checks Belinda had cashed and seeing the stark, simple life the Murdocks led, he'd had to face the fact that he'd been wrong.

"You say you divided the work responsibilities after Tomas died. How were things around here while he was still living?"

She smiled and her green eyes sparkled with fond memories of happier times. "It was very different. Daddy usually had no fewer than five wranglers hired to work the place. Not to say that Rose and I didn't work back then. We did. But we could choose our own hours and set our own pace."

"You had to let all the cowboys go?"

Nodding sadly, she looked away from him. "It's not something I like to think about. This ranch used to employ five men who counted on their salaries to provide for their families. It was…"

She paused and Wyatt could see her throat working as she tried to swallow. The sight so unsettled him, he had to glance away.

"It was very hard when we had to tell them we couldn't use them anymore," she finally finished.

Wyatt suddenly thought of all the men he'd fired for different reasons down through the years and how impersonal those decisions had been to him. Yet to Chloe, letting the wranglers go had been like saying goodbye to a part of her family.

Had being an oilman for so many years left him without a heart? Or did Chloe have too much of one? He didn't know. But one thing was for sure, she was making him look at life from an altogether different angle.

Something, he wasn't quite sure what, made him reach over and cover her hand with his. "Maybe it will be like that again, someday, Chloe. I hope it is."

Perhaps she was a fool, but she honestly believed he meant that. The idea he might have even a small measure of compassion for her disturbed Chloe. She didn't want him to care for her. She didn't want him to give her a reason to like him, to soften her heart toward him.

"I…" Her eyes fell from his to the tabletop. "I… uh…I'm going to try my best to make it that way…again." Her eyes lifted slowly back to his. "It will probably take years. But time is one thing I do have. And energy," she added with a little joke of a smile.

But how long would her energy last? he wondered solemnly. How long would it be before this place broke her down and turned her into a tired, bitter woman?

For Chloe, the touch of his hand was growing hotter and

hotter, leading her thoughts to places she shouldn't dare think about.

Gently, but firmly, she pulled her hand away and stood. "Thanks for the coffee. I'd better get the twins to bed now."

Wyatt knew she was bothered by his touching her. So was he. Bothered because he couldn't get enough of it. And he knew from now until the time he left this ranch, it was going to be a struggle with himself to keep his hands off her.

Rising to his feet, he drained the last of his coffee. "I'd better come with you so I can learn all about bedding a baby. I have a feeling there's more to it than just laying them in the crib and covering them up."

He followed her out of the room and Chloe breathed in several long breaths. She had to keep her senses straight, she had to remember who he was and why he was here.

In the living room they each picked up a sleeping twin and carried them to the nursery. A single bed was positioned at one end of the small room. Chloe placed Anna on the mattress and motioned for Wyatt to do the same with Adam.

"We need to put on their nightclothes before we put them in the cribs," she explained.

Her voice was normal, not hushed and Wyatt glanced at the sleeping twins expecting them to start howling at any moment.

"You're going to wake them up," he whispered.

Chloe smiled knowingly. "By this time at night they're tuckered out. It would take a freight train to rouse them."

She pulled footed pajamas out of a nearby chest of drawers, then pointed to a stack of diapers on a small dressing table. "Those are the regular diapers you've been using today. The heavy ones for overnight are here in the closet," she told him.

He moved to where she stood by the open door and

peered over her shoulder. She smelled like a garden of roses on a hot summer's day. Sweet, warm and seductive. The scent filled his head with erotic images, and his hand itched to slip the clasp from her hair and watch it tumble down onto her shoulders. It would be so good to take her by the shoulders and pull her close.

"Yes. I see."

Something about the huskiness in his voice drew Chloe back around and her breath caught in her throat as she looked up at him. There was a softness in his gray eyes, a warmth that stirred the woman deep inside her.

He'd promised not to kiss her again. Not to repeat what had happened in the kitchen this morning. At the moment, the promise had relieved her. Now it was vaguely disappointing to know she might never again feel his lips against hers.

Clearing her throat, she started to step around him, but his hand quickly caught her by the shoulder.

"Wyatt—"

"Don't worry. I'm not about to ravish you."

The mere idea of Wyatt ravishing her was enough to send heat hurtling through her body like an atomic explosion.

"I didn't think you were," she murmured.

His mouth twisted wryly. "But the idea crossed your mind."

Her heart was thumping so hard she felt light-headed. "Are you telling me it hasn't crossed yours?" she asked boldly.

"It's crossed it so many times, the inside of my forehead looks like a roadmap," he confessed. "But I gave you my promise."

"Is your word good?"

His fingers slid ever so gently up the slope of her shoulder until they reached her hair.

"I've never broken a promise before." But then he'd never been so tempted before either, he realized.

Her nerves buzzing, her mouth dry, she closed her eyes as his strong fingers combed slowly through her hair. He was attracted to her. No, it was more than that, she reasoned. He wanted to make love to her. She could see it in his eyes, feel it in his touch. The idea both thrilled and terrified her.

"Wyatt, we—"

"I know," he interrupted. "We shouldn't be getting this close to each other."

"I'm not a fool, Wyatt." She opened her eyes and looked at him. "We're two very different people. Back in Houston you would have never looked at a woman like me."

"A woman like you?" His brows lifted. "Chloe, there are no women like you back in Houston."

"Oh, there are, Wyatt. You just don't move in their circles."

It was on the tip of his tongue to tell her she was wrong. There wasn't anybody else in the world like her. But that would be like admitting he was falling in love with her. And he wasn't. He just had a case of healthy lust for Chloe Murdock.

"You make me sound like a snob. I may know a lot of upper-class people. But that doesn't mean I associate strictly with those kind."

To make her point, Chloe lifted her hands and offered them to him. "Look Wyatt. Don't tell me you've ever asked a woman with hands like these out on a date."

He took hold of her small, work-worn hands. The nails were clipped to a short, practical length. They were bare of polish, the cuticles ragged in places. He turned the palms up and ran his thumbs over the calluses lying just below her fingers.

She was right in a way, he silently mused. Her hands

weren't soft or jeweled or manicured like those of the women he knew. But they were far more beautiful to him. He didn't know exactly why. He only knew that when he watched her touch the twins and even her horses, she did it with love.

Bending his head, he placed a kiss on each palm, then looked up at her. "You're wrong to belittle yourself, Chloe."

Her lips twisted mockingly, while inside her heart was filled with painful regret. "Weren't you trying to do just that when you first came here?"

Rueful shadows filled his eyes. "That already seems like a long time ago, Chloe," he murmured. "And if I looked down on you then, it was only because I was angry and hurting. I didn't know you."

"You don't know me now," she reminded him.

His brow furrowed. "Why do you say that, Chloe? Is there something about you you're not telling me?"

A dark, closed shutter fell over Chloe's face and without answering, she stepped around him and moved back to where the twins lay sleeping on the narrow bed. Wyatt followed.

"Talk to me, Chloe."

"I am what you see, Wyatt. I'm not for you and you're not for me. Don't complicate things by being—"

She didn't know how to finish. He did it for her. "Attracted to you?"

He was standing just inches behind her and Chloe was so very tempted to turn to him, to tell him all the hidden things in her heart and hope he would understand. But he wouldn't. Richard had professed to love her. He'd even wanted to marry her. Until he'd found out she was barren. Then she hadn't been good enough for him. It would be the same with Wyatt. He was a man accustomed to the best of things. He wouldn't hold on to anything flawed.

"I guess that's what I'm trying to say," she mumbled.

Chloe was right, he supposed. They were two very different people. He had a life in Houston he would soon have to go back to. He couldn't let himself become involved with her. And why, oh why, did he even want to?

"Why does that bother you?" he asked her. "Is it me or just men in general?"

She turned around and stared at him with eyes so sad and accusing Wyatt felt something inside him wither.

"Have you forgotten why you're here, Wyatt?"

His sister's death. Her plea for him to get the twins. And his silent vow to do so. He'd started to New Mexico with all those reasons sharp and clear in his mind. But when he looked at Chloe nothing was clear or simple. Except that he wanted her.

"I'm here to help you with the twins," he finally replied.

Her jaw hardened. "No. You're here to *get* the twins."

Until this very moment, Wyatt hadn't really understood what that meant to Chloe and how, in the deepest part of her, she must hate him for wanting to take her babies. But they weren't her babies really. They were Belinda's.

"Is that all you see when you look at me?" he asked, his voice rough with frustration. "Just the enemy?"

It wasn't. But Chloe knew the smart thing to do would be to let him think so. Things were quickly getting out of hand between them and it looked as though it was going to be left up to her to put a stop to it.

"I can't let myself forget who you are, Wyatt." Grim faced, she turned back to the babies and reached for their pajamas. "I told you before. The twins mean more to me than anything. I won't let you or anyone come between us."

Was he trying to come between Chloe and the babies? Wyatt asked himself. Was he wanting her love or the twins, or both? And what the hell was he going to do about any of it?

Chapter Nine

Almost a week later, Wyatt entered the study and found Chloe posting bills in the ledger. The banker's lamp cast a soft glow over her pale features and auburn hair. Her gaze was fixed in deep concentration on the figures before her. She was unaware of Wyatt's presence until he stood directly in front of her.

Lifting her head, she said nothing, just looked at him.

"I saw the light. I thought you'd already gone to bed."

What was the point in going to bed? Chloe thought. She couldn't sleep. Working on the ledger was more productive than lying in bed thinking about him—something she'd been doing constantly for the past week.

"I wanted to get this paperwork done first," she told him.

Rose and Justine and their families had left the house only a little more than an hour ago. They'd brought a potluck supper and stayed several hours afterwards.

During the last few days Wyatt had met Chloe's relatives. One by one he'd decided he liked them all. Roy and Harlan were fair, friendly men and both interesting to talk to. Rose and Justine were each straightforward, intelligent and beautiful. But the thing that had struck Wyatt the most about the two women was their kindness and willingness to accept him as the twins' uncle—rather than a rattlesnake just waiting to strike, as Chloe seemed to regard him.

Dropping her head, Chloe went back to work on the ledger, and Wyatt knew she was telling him to leave her alone. But so far he hadn't made it a habit to follow her wishes.

Propping his thigh on the corner of the desk, he said, "Rose left us all her meatballs. She said she knew you wouldn't cook unless you had to."

"She knows me."

It was all Wyatt could do not to reach over and close the book. She'd been cool to him all week and he was finally at the simmering point.

"If you're worried I've been putting my long-distance calls on your telephone line, don't be. I have a company calling card."

"I didn't realize you'd been making any calls."

Who was she kidding? She'd walked into this study several times and seen him on the telephone. Each time she had immediately whirled on her bootheel and left the room. "You've seen me on the telephone. Who the hell did you think I was talking to?"

The roughness of his voice grabbed her attention. She looked up at him. "I don't really care who you call or if you bill it all to the Bar M," she said dryly. "The ranch is already broke. What's a few more hundred dollars in phone bills?"

Wyatt understood she had plenty to worry about. Since he'd always had money, it was hard for him to imagine the stress of trying to meet bills without it. Still, he didn't want to be her whipping boy.

"Why are you being so snotty?"

It was all Chloe could do to keep from jumping to her

feet and yelling at him to get out and leave her alone. "Who's being snotty? You were the one cursing."

Sighing, he stood and jammed his hands in his jean pockets.

"Well, so I was," he said, his voice dripping with sarcasm, then fixing his eyes on hers, he added, "Your sisters don't seem to have any trouble being kind to me. I wonder why you do?"

Snorting, she jumped to her feet. "Is that what you want from me, Wyatt? My kindness? I thought it was my babies."

Suddenly the room was horribly quiet. Wyatt felt as if she'd flung a knife into his chest. "Why are you doing this? The day of Kitty's accident, you welcomed my help. You told me how much you appreciated my being here. And you were pleasant to be around. Now you look at me as if I were a leper."

Even though the room was mostly dark, Chloe could see his face. The pain she saw there matched the agony in her heart. He was right. She had avoided him as much as possible. But he'd left her little choice. It was either that or make a complete fool of herself.

"I don't look at you like you're a leper. I'm just keeping a safe distance," she said in a low, desperate voice, then turning her back to him she walked over to the wall of windows looking out toward the mountains. "And don't ask me why. You know why."

Infuriated by her attitude, he went to her.

"Because you're afraid of me? Or more afraid of yourself?" he asked, standing just inches behind her back.

Goaded by his questions, she whirled around. "I'm not afraid of you! I'm not afraid of any man!"

"Then you're afraid of yourself. You think I might tempt you to give in and act like a real woman for once in your life."

All the pent-up pain and frustration inside Chloe came

pouring out. She flew at him with both fists and pounded his chest as though it was a dirty saddle blanket needing to be cleaned.

Wyatt was stunned motionless by her flogging. But after a moment he decided she'd vented enough anger on him. Grabbing both her wrists, he held her tight.

Chloe struggled against him, then realized she was wasting her strength trying to overpower him. Flinging her hair back out of her eyes, she glared up at him.

"How dare you say something like that to me!"

"Why?" he asked. "Because it's true?"

"Do you think you're so irresistible that I'm actually going around aching for you?"

"Yes," he said with quiet conviction. "Because I've been aching for you."

Something inside her crumbled, and she had to look away as tears filled her eyes.

"You don't mean that, Wyatt. Not really."

Moving closer, he placed his hand on her shoulder. "Surely that doesn't surprise you. The first night I stayed under this roof I admitted I was attracted to you. Did you think that was going to change?"

Her head bobbed up and down. "Yes. After you got to know me."

And she'd been trying to show him the very worst of herself. Why? he wondered. What was she really afraid of?

With a groan of frustration, he said, "Hell, you won't let me get to know you. But this icy act of yours hasn't changed the way I feel whenever I look at you. And that is what you've been trying to do, isn't it? Cool me down? Make me dislike you?"

"Wyatt, the twins—"

"Yes, I know I came here because of the twins. But you can't deny there's something between us. Why won't you admit it?"

Groaning, she moved to step past him. Wyatt grabbed her by the upper arms.

"Wyatt, you promised you wouldn't kiss me again."

Her words were urging him to keep that promise, yet the smoldering light in her eyes was begging him to break it.

"And I haven't," he said, "I just want us to be... friends, at least."

"You think we were becoming friends?" His assumption surprised Chloe. She didn't think Wyatt had felt connected to her in any way.

His hands moved down her arms until his fingers were curled around both wrists. "Isn't that what you would call us?"

A friend had never kissed her the way Wyatt had. A friend had never made her feel so hot and shaky and reckless she couldn't trust herself to look at him.

"I don't think you and I could ever be friends, Wyatt. We seem to bring out the...worst in each other."

His hands slid slowly, warmly, up her arms until they were resting around the base of her neck. Beneath his fingers, he could feel her pulse throbbing wildly, the satin smoothness of her bare skin. And his throat tightened with a longing he couldn't understand or explain.

"You call that the worst, Chloe? You think it's bad for a man and woman to want each other?"

"It is when the man and woman are you and me."

The past few days Wyatt had spent living here with Chloe had been the hardest, yet the most fulfilling time in his life. He'd found out about babies and all it took to care for them. He'd learned a little about ranching and raising horses and what it was like to live in the mountains of New Mexico. But most of all, he'd learned about family and about love. And how it felt to have neither.

"Chloe, God knows I didn't come here to fall in love with you. But I believe I have."

She began to tremble. Not just from the shock of his words, but because she feared they echoed what was in her own heart. Oh, dear God, she silently prayed, why had this happened?

"Wyatt...don't say that to me," she whispered desperately.

"I have to, Chloe. I can't stand your being around me, but not being near me. Do you understand what I'm trying to say?"

Yes, she did. She'd missed the closeness they'd shared that first night he was here. A hundred times a day she had to stop herself from going to him just to hear his voice or see his smile. Over and over she found herself wanting to share things with him. Yet she'd held back, knowing it would be disastrous to allow herself to get attached to him.

"I do understand, Wyatt. And I know I've... behaved..." she drew in a deep breath and let it out "...like I don't have good sense. But I..." she spread her palms against his warm chest "...I'm afraid. When I talked about you not knowing me. What I meant..." Her throat closed around the rest of the words. She turned away from him and swallowed at the tightness, but still she was unable to utter a sound.

"Chloe," he whispered, his arms sliding around her waist. "If you've been hurt by a man in the past, I can understand you being afraid to jump into another relationship. Hell, I've had some pretty stinking affairs myself. But that doesn't mean I'm going to deliberately hurt you."

Had he gone insane? He could hurt her in a thousand ways! She tried to harden herself, to tell her heart not to cry and shatter like a piece of fragile crystal.

"Have you ever loved a woman, planned to marry and spend your whole life with her, and then have her tell you it was over? That you just weren't good enough for her?"

Her husky voice was full of pain and resentment. Wyatt bent his head and pressed the side of his face next to hers.

"I can honestly say I've never been in love, Chloe. In lust, maybe. Or infatuated. But love? I've always doubted its existence. At least the earth-moving kind that you see in movies or hear friends talk about. I didn't think it was possible for anyone to care about another human being more than he cared for himself. But I do care for you, Chloe."

Her heart throbbed with exhilaration. Yet at the same time it was filled with pain.

"That's what he said, too. And I thought he meant it. I still think Richard did care for me up to a point. But I'm an honest woman, Wyatt. I've told you that before. And in this case my honesty was more than he could take."

Sensing her torment, he tightened his arms around her waist. "I can't imagine you having a sordid past. But I wouldn't hold it against you if you did."

A sarcastic laugh spilled from Chloe's lips. "Other than Richard I've only had a handful of boyfriends. A past I do not have. Just a condition. I can't have children."

Never had any words hit Wyatt so hard. Naturally, he'd been shocked when he'd heard his father had been killed in an accident and equally stunned when he'd been notified of Belinda's death. But Wyatt was a realist, and no one knew better than he that death knew no age or social standing. It just happened. Yet hearing Chloe was sterile was like a fist in the face.

She was so incredibly young, so full of beauty and sexual vibrance. It saddened him terribly to think making love for Chloe would always be just that. It would never have the added wonder of conceiving a child.

"I don't know what to say, Chloe."

"That's funny. Richard knew all sorts of things to say. How sorry he was. How unfair it was for me."

"It is sad and unfair," Wyatt agreed.

She moved away from him and Wyatt watched as she

leaned her forehead against the windowpane and stared pensively out at the night sky.

"You think I wanted to hear that from him?"

Wyatt didn't answer. He wasn't thinking about her condition now. He was suddenly overwhelmed with jealousy as he tried to imagine this unknown man who had once captured Chloe's heart.

"I don't know."

Her gaze jerked over to him. "No. I didn't figure you would know," she said dryly.

He turned his palms up in a helpless gesture. "Look, Chloe, maybe you have this idea that I'm a playboy or something. Maybe you think I've had lots of women in my life. But that isn't the case. I know all about getting oil or gas out of the ground, what it takes to get it refined and distributed. I could go out on a rig right now and work the floor, the derrick, the generators, anything you asked me to do, I could do it. If I had to fly to Saudi Arabia tomorrow and make a business deal for several thousand barrels of oil, I would know how to do that, too. But I don't know all about women. I don't always know what they want to hear from a man when they're hurting or sad."

She looked back toward the windows and sighed. There wasn't any reason for her to be bitter with Wyatt. He wasn't the man who'd jilted her. But he would, she knew, if given the same situation.

"I'm sorry, Wyatt. I didn't mean to get into all this." Biting down on her lip, she glanced at him. "I never wanted you to know about any of this."

Something in her face urged him to cross the few steps separating them. "Why?"

She didn't answer immediately. Wyatt slid his fingers into her hair and against her scalp. "Tell me," he whispered.

"Because I didn't want to use it as one more argument

to keep the twins. If I could have ten children of my own, I would still want the twins. So my condition is inconsequential.''

Maybe she wanted to think so. But how could it be? Wyatt wondered. "Is that the only reason?"

Suddenly she turned, then burying her face in his chest, began to quietly sob. And like snow on a spring day, his heart melted and filled with a desperate need to comfort the woman in his arms.

"I didn't want you to know…because I—I didn't want you to think of me as half a woman."

Closing his eyes, Wyatt pressed his cheek against the top of her head. "Your inability to have children has nothing to do with your womanhood. You're the sexiest woman I've ever known."

Sniffing, she shook her head. "That isn't enough for most men."

"Is that what this Richard told you?"

"More or less." She lifted teary green eyes to his. "You see, at the time we were dating he was acquiring a degree in political science. He had dreams of running for a state office and eventually for governor of New Mexico. And, of course, the correct image for a politician is a wife and children."

"You could have adopted," Wyatt reasoned.

Her laugh was laced with acid. "That wasn't what Richard wanted for himself. And who could blame him?"

Wyatt could. But deep down he was damn glad the bastard had been too selfishly absorbed with his own career to realize what he was losing in Chloe.

"You know what I think, Chloe? I think you made a lucky escape. You would have had a miserable life with a politician. Especially one who didn't love you. And he didn't, you know."

He was right. But no matter how you reasoned rejection, it was still a bitter pill to swallow. "Don't tell me it wouldn't matter to you that a woman you wanted to marry couldn't have children, Wyatt. We both would know you'd be lying.''

''I'm not going to tell you it wouldn't matter. Of course it would. Most people do want children of their own. But I wouldn't give up a woman I loved just because she couldn't get pregnant. There's more to a marriage than just having kids. At least, I think there is.''

''Are you saying this to make me feel better about myself, or to make me see reason about you taking the twins?''

Dear God, he'd been so caught up in his feelings for Chloe, he'd forgotten about the twins. How could he think about taking them to Houston now? How could he think about going himself?

''I'm...I don't want to talk about the twins tonight, Chloe. This is just about you and me.''

He was still on that? After all she'd told him? ''There is no me and you, Wyatt. There never could be.''

His features grew soft as his eyes glided over her precious face. ''How can you be so sure of that?'' he asked huskily.

''You're Belinda Waller's brother,'' she said, but deep inside, Chloe knew that no longer meant anything.

''And you're Tomas Murdock's daughter. But neither one of us can help that.''

''Maybe we can't help it,'' Chloe said, ''but we can't forget it, either.''

The breaking point for Wyatt had finally come. ''Maybe not,'' he said gruffly, ''but can you forget this?''

Chloe saw his face drawing down to hers, yet she couldn't move her head, or pull away. She was like a piece of steel clinging helplessly to a magnet.

''Wyatt,'' she breathed in protest, then sighed as his lips settled over hers.

She'd wanted this man all week and all week she'd re-

sisted letting him know. But tonight her will to keep him
at bay had broken. She'd told him she was barren, yet here
he was holding her, kissing her as though she was all he
would ever want. The idea left her as giddy as the drugging
taste of his lips.

"Chloe, who we are or what we are doesn't matter. This
is all that matters."

Her body in total agreement, she clutched his shoulders
and her head fell back as he planted a row of kisses down
her neck, then lower to where her sweater veed at the
valley between her breasts.

A firestorm was ripping through Wyatt, blanking his
mind of everything except the need to have her. Making
short work of the buttons on her sweater, he quickly
shoved it off her shoulders and down her arms.

Her breasts were encased in bright red lace. The sensual
color was an intoxicating sight against her white skin and
he groaned as he dipped his head and suckled first one
nipple and then the other.

The thin barrier of lace did little to dull the sweet, soft
taste of her. Like a drink of straight bourbon, it shot to
Wyatt's head, fuzzed his thinking and filled him with heat.

Clutching her bottom with both hands he pulled her hips
tight against the ache of his arousal and Chloe moaned at
the onslaught of sensations rushing through her. She'd
never wanted any man like this. She hadn't known she
could want a man this badly.

Bending, Wyatt slipped an arm beneath the back of her
knees and carried her to a small sofa at one end of the
room and gently deposited her on the cushions. Then lying
down beside her, he took her in his arms and ravaged her
mouth with another hungry kiss.

Wave after wave of desire washed over Chloe, urging
her to press her body against the hard length of his, spread
her fingers against the back of his scalp and hold his mouth
fast to hers.

Not until they were both starving for air did the kiss end, but as far as Wyatt was concerned his thirst for her hadn't nearly been quenched.

"I've never wanted any woman like this, Chloe," he murmured against her ear. "I don't understand it, but you've done something to me."

Wyatt had done something to her, too, Chloe thought with sudden clarity. He'd given her a glimpse of all that she'd been missing in her life, all the things she would miss in the future without a husband to love her, fulfill her, to simply be a part of her.

As Wyatt's hand slipped up the warm curve of her thigh, Chloe wanted nothing more than to make love to him. But where would that leave her? What would it mean, if anything, after the flame between them had cooled? He was going back to Houston, and she had a ranch to run. And the twins. Dear Lord, even in this moment of passion she couldn't forget them.

Her hands bracketing both sides of his face, she lifted his head and looked at him with pleading eyes. "Wyatt, we have to stop," she whispered. "Don't make me want you like this. I can't—"

She stopped as tears began to slip from the corners of her eyes and roll down her cheeks. Her anguish tore a hole right through his heart and Wyatt knew in that moment he could never do anything to hurt Chloe. He wanted to protect her, cherish her, make sure she never cried another tear. But how would he ever be able to convince her of that?

"Chloe, I thought this was what you wanted."

She moaned with sheer hopelessness. "Dammit, Wyatt, I do want it. That's what makes it..." A sob clogged her throat, and she jumped to her feet before he could stop her. "That's what makes it so awful."

Sobbing, she whirled and ran from the room. Wyatt stared after her, his body aching, his thoughts whirling.

His first impulse was to go after her, but then he heard the door to her bedroom slam shut and knew there would be no reasoning with her tonight.

He would have to begin all over again tomorrow, he decided, and hope that she would soon grow to trust him.

By the next morning the weather had taken a bitter turn. Rain blew in from the north drenching the ranch and making it impossible for Chloe to gallop any of her horses.

When Rose arrived at nine, Chloe was sitting on a wooden keg outside the tack room door. Her gloved hands were cradling a thermos cup of coffee and her nose and cheeks were red from the cold.

"What a morning!" Rose exclaimed. She took off her yellow slicker, **gave** it a hard shake, then pulled it back over her heavy work clothes. "I nearly didn't make it over the river. The water is almost over the bridge. And to think a few months ago everything around here was dying from lack of rain."

"Do you want some coffee?" Chloe offered her sister. "There's plenty more where this came from."

"No. I just stopped by a minute to see you before I went on up to the cattle barn."

She eased down on an overturned feed bucket leaning against the wall. Water was still running in rivulets from her slicker and hat, and her boots looked as though she'd just waded across the Hondo River. But there was a smile on her face, and her cheerfulness almost made Chloe ashamed of her own gloomy mood.

"Well, the rain has put a damper on my work," Chloe said. "But I guess it'll give me a chance to clean out the rest of the stalls this morning."

Rose's gaze slipped over Chloe's shadowed face. "You look exhausted. Didn't you get any rest last night?"

Rest? How did a person rest once they'd had a fire built

inside them? Chloe wondered. Aloud, she said, "Not much."

Rose pulled out a handkerchief and mopped her wet face. "You were awfully quiet last night. Are you still worrying about Wyatt?"

Chloe's eyes narrowed at her sister. "What do you mean?"

Rose made an impatient swipe through the air with her hand. "You know what I mean. About his taking the twins. Why else would you be worrying about him?"

Chloe opened her mouth, closed it, then decided Rose was the most understanding, open-minded one of the whole family. If she could talk to anyone, it was Rose.

With a grimace on her face, Chloe said, "I guess you haven't noticed there's, uh...friction between us."

Rose's brows lifted. "Friction? I thought you were glad he was helping you out."

"I was. I am. I mean, oh, dammit, Rose, Wyatt says he thinks he's in love with me."

Her expression barely flickering, Rose continued to study her sister. "And how do you feel about him?"

Chloe groaned. "Does that really matter? Surely you can see the absurdity of it?"

"There's nothing absurd about two people loving each other. Believe me, Chloe, now that I have Harlan I can tell you how precious love is."

Chloe glanced away from her sister as pain filled her chest. Rose was so very happy now. And Justine was blooming with child. There was no sense in denying she wanted what her sisters had. But she wasn't fool enough to expect to find it with Wyatt.

"I didn't say I loved Wyatt."

"No. You didn't. But I can see you're in agony and nothing can put a look like that on a woman's face except loving a man when she doesn't want to."

Trying her best to appear impassive, Chloe tossed away

the last of her coffee and tightened the lid back on the thermos. "I've only known Wyatt for a couple of weeks. How could I be in love with him?"

Rose chuckled knowingly. "I think I fell in love with Harlan the first night I talked to him. It just took me awhile to realize it."

Chloe let out a long breath. "Wyatt isn't like us, Rose. He lives in a condominium in Houston, for goodness sake. He deals in oil like Daddy used to deal in livestock."

A lopsided smile touched Rose's face. "Maybe that's why you love him. Because he's a little like Daddy."

"No!" Chloe frowned at her. "He's nothing like him. He's not a rancher. He's an oilman."

"So he is. But he's got the same drive and ambition. And the same fairness, I think. Otherwise, he would have already taken you to court over the twins."

Chloe speared a hand through her auburn hair. "The twins. That's another thing. Who's to say he isn't trying to get to me to clear his way to the twins?"

"He didn't have to tell you he loved you," Rose reasoned.

Chloe got to her feet. "No. But you and I both know that some men will spout anything just to get what they want. And I've got to remember that Wyatt came here for the twins. And it's most likely the twins he's still after."

Rose got to her feet and fished a pair of dry leather gloves from her slicker pocket. As she pulled them on she said, "Chloe, you've grown so bitter it scares me."

A spurt of anger shot through Chloe. "Hellfire, Rose, don't you think I have a right to be?"

Rose stepped over to her sister and laid her hand gently alongside Chloe's cheek.

"You also have a right to be happy, sis. Please think about that."

Happy? She was falling in love with a man she could

never have. A man who had the power to take away all she'd ever wanted in life. That didn't sound like happiness to her. It was pure hell.

Chapter Ten

"**W**yatt, darling, I really think I ought to send a psychiatrist, or at least a therapist out there to check on you. You've definitely slipped a cog or two. Have you forgotten you have a job, an oil company to run back in Houston?"

Wyatt frowned at Sandra's inane question. "I know perfectly well what I have in Houston. I have capable people working for me. And if I'm needed all they have to do is pick up the phone to get me."

"Well, I'm not so sure I'd like being that dispensable. Besides, what in the world were you thinking agreeing to be a baby-sitter and cook for those people? It's incredible! Don't you remember you went there to *get* the twins? Not to be their nanny! I thought you'd already be back home with them by now."

Wyatt had planned to be away from here sooner, too. But things had changed since he'd come to New Mexico. A lot of things. "I know, Sandra. But Chloe was in a bad spot with her aunt being down for a while. And I felt it was the decent thing for me to do."

"Decent? Your sister wanted you to get her babies. Apparently she didn't think the Murdocks were fit to raise them.''

Wyatt cringed and closed his eyes. "My sister was not altogether sane when she wrote that letter, Sandra."

He could hear her sharply indrawn breath. "Wyatt! That's an awful thing to say. I thought you loved Belinda."

Wyatt drummed his fingers against the desktop. He'd always been able to talk to Sandra before about things. She was a good listener and looked at things realistically. Or so he'd thought. Now he felt like a fool or a masochist for even calling her. And if he hadn't been so damn torn over Chloe, he wouldn't have.

"I did love her, Sandra. Very much. But that doesn't mean I'm blind to her faults. Since I've come here I've found out she was...in far more trouble than I could have imagined. And as for the Murdocks, the only one of them she knew was Tomas. So she could hardly know if they were fit to raise the twins.''

As he waited for her to reply, he could hear Mozart on the CD player in her living room. Sandra only listened to the classics. But so did he, now. The only music on the Bar M was a radio in the kitchen and the nearest radio station that could be picked up without too much static played pure classics. George Jones, Hank Thompson, Carl Smith. He was even becoming addicted to Patsy Cline.

"Okay, so your sister was having some problems. That doesn't mean you owe the Murdocks your help or anything else. I think that high mountain air is starving your brain for oxygen. You can't think straight."

As far as Wyatt was concerned he was thinking more clearly than he ever had and seeing things he'd never taken the time to see before.

"I know what I'm doing," he said while rubbing a finger over his furrowed brow.

Sandra's shrill laugh was full of disbelief. "Just what

are you doing, Wyatt? Learning how to be a 'daddy,' or letting these people use you?''

Suddenly the image of Chloe, the babies and the rest of her family laughing and talking around the fireplace filled Wyatt's head. Yes, he'd been used before. And maybe he was setting himself up to be taken. But he was beginning to see that being rich didn't necessarily mean having money. Sandra wouldn't understand that. But Wyatt did. Now.

''Maybe. And maybe I'm just learning how to be a human being.''

''Wyatt—'' she began to scold only to have Wyatt cut her off.

''I've got to go, Sandra. Anna's crying.''

On the way to the nursery, he met Chloe in the hallway. Anna was cuddled in her arms. The baby was cooing happily and tugging on a strand of Chloe's hair.

''What are you doing coming back to the house this early?'' he asked, glancing at his wristwatch. ''It's only ten.''

''Rose sent me after more coffee.''

She walked past him toward the kitchen. Wyatt followed, his eyes on her curvy little bottom encased in faded denim and outlined with a pair of worn leather chaps. Her boots were muddy and her hair was damp. She smelled like wind and rain and he longed to take her in his arms and kiss the cold from her face.

''I didn't hear you come in. I was on the telephone.''

She put Anna in a high chair and gave her a rubber teething ring.

''Distributing oil and gas already this morning?''

Since he'd been staying here on the ranch, she'd rarely asked him about his job. It surprised Wyatt that she did now.

''No. Talking to a friend.''

She went to the cabinet and began putting on a fresh pot of coffee. Wyatt went over and took hold of her arm.

"What are you doing?" she asked sharply, her senses on instant alert.

"I want you to sit down while I make the coffee."

"Oh," she murmured, her face flushing with embarrassment. She knew it was crazy of her to be leery of his every move, but after tasting the heat of his ardor last night, she knew how quickly passion could flare between them. She couldn't let it happen again. Next time she might not have enough willpower to resist him.

She settled into a chair at the end of the table and watched him as he measured coffee grounds and water. "I suppose you're missing all your friends back in Houston."

He thought about her assumption as he flipped the switch on the coffeemaker and walked over to her. "I don't really have that many friends. Or at least friends as you would call them. There're a few co-workers I'm close to. But only at work. I guess I haven't taken the time to do a lot of socializing."

"Socializing isn't the same as being with friends," she told him.

He grinned and the sight of his white teeth and crinkled eyes filled her with uncommon heat. She didn't know why he looked so good to her. He wasn't exactly a beautiful man. And he certainly wasn't the cowboy type she usually associated with. But damned if he wasn't the sexiest male she'd ever been around with his black hair, dark skin and cloud gray eyes. And the way he kissed her was sinful and scary and she didn't know how she was going to be able to keep on living here with him and keep her wits about her.

"I know what you mean," he said. "While my Dad was still living he used to throw lots of parties for fellow businessmen. I never got so sick of mixing and mingling and saying nice things just because it was the profitable thing to do. Now the guys out on the rigs who I called my friends were a different matter. I could and did say anything to them." His grin turned lopsided and a bit wistful. "I guess I sort of miss those old days when I was still working out in the field. And Dad was still around."

Up until now, Wyatt hadn't mentioned his father or his personal life all that much. She figured there was still a part of him that blamed the Murdocks for his sister's death and Chloe was the last person he wanted to share himself with. Yet there was so much she longed to know about him.

"What exactly happened to your father, Wyatt? Did he die suddenly?"

Glancing at the coffeemaker he saw the carafe was full. Walking over to the cabinet, he took the lid off the empty thermos, then filled it with the hot brew.

"My father had flown out to an offshore drilling rig in a helicopter and was trying to get back to the mainland when an unexpected storm blew in. He and the pilot were both killed in the crash. He was only fifty-three when it happened."

There wasn't much to read on his face as he carried the thermos to her, but she'd heard the loss in his voice and it touched her more deeply than she cared to admit. "Did you—were you close to him?"

She took the thermos from him but didn't hurry to her feet.

He said, "When you talk about having friends, Chloe, I guess my father was the best friend I ever had."

Her eyes shadowed with lingering grief, she nodded. "My father was the best friend I ever had, too. Justine and Rose loved Daddy, but I was the one closest to him." Sighing, she rose slowly to her feet. "You know, of all the problems we've had here on the ranch, none of them compare to losing him. "I...don't think I'll ever stop missing him."

Wyatt gently touched her cheek. "No. You won't ever

stop missing him completely. But the pain of it will get better with time. Believe me.''

The fact that he was trying to comfort her, even in this small way, went straight to Chloe's heart. Since he'd first come here, she tried to convince herself he was a materialistic man without much compassion for anyone. Maybe she was wrong. Maybe he could be falling in love with her. The idea left her trembling inside.

Glancing over at Anna, she murmured in a husky voice, ''Some people might think I'm crazy, but I thank God everyday for letting Daddy have the twins. He's a part of them and I cherish that.'' Clearing her throat, she looked at him and added, ''But I suppose you look at them and see Belinda.''

Funny, but he didn't. Maybe that was because the babies looked so much like Chloe and her sisters and nothing like Belinda. Or maybe he'd just never been close enough to Belinda to feel a spiritual connection with her and the twins.

''When I look at the twins I see you, Chloe.''

The simple words shook her to the very core of her being. ''Are you being...honest with me?''

He inclined his head toward Anna. ''Look at that baby.''

Chloe grimaced. ''I'm not talking about physical appearance.''

He shook his head. ''I'm not either. True, I came here because of Belinda and because she wanted me to get the twins. But now that I've gotten to know them I...don't see my sister. God help her now. I see you. And me.'' She sucked in a breath as he took a gentle hold on her shoulders. ''I happen to think the twins need a mother and a father.''

Everything inside her went stock-still. Did he mean him and her? Raising the twins together? No! It would never work. She couldn't deal with that idea at all!

Clutching the thermos, she pulled away from him and

started out of the room. "I...uh...Rose is waiting on me, and I've got lots to do." Pausing at the door, she forced herself to glance over her shoulder at him. He was watching her intently and the close scrutiny of his gray eyes set her pulse to pounding. "I'm going to try to be back in early for lunch. I need to drive in to Ruidoso and do some...banking business."

In other words, she needed money, Wyatt thought. "I'll go with you."

She shook her head. "A bank is no place for two babies. You'll be chasing them all over the lobby. Besides, there's nothing you can do."

"I don't know about that. I usually have quite a bit of influence on bankers. Especially with loan officers."

Her brows shot upward. "How do you know I'm not going there to make a deposit?"

He didn't want to be flip. Not when he knew she was consumed with worry over the ranch's welfare. But to help her in any way, he had to be honest. "Where would you have gotten anything around here to deposit? As far as I know you and Rose haven't sold any livestock."

He was too observant for his own good, Chloe thought with frustration. "We could. If we...had to."

"I understand that. I'm just asking where you got any money to make a deposit."

Stamping her foot, she glared at him. "Dammit, Wyatt. This is none of your business."

He quickly went over to her and took the thermos from her hands. "I'm going down to the barn and get Rose. She can watch the twins while you and I drive into the bank in Ruidoso."

"She has work to do!" Chloe exclaimed.

"You can help her with it later. Now go." He nudged her in the direction of the hallway. "If you hurry we can get there before lunchtime."

* * *

Thirty minutes later they were on their way to Ruidoso in Wyatt's plush sedan. As Chloe stared out at the misty clouds hanging over the mountains, she wondered what Rose was thinking back at the ranch and wondered, too, what Wyatt was really doing coming with her to the bank like this. Maybe he thought she'd been lying about her troubled finances all this time. Perhaps he believed Belinda hadn't really taken their money and he could find out the truth by tagging along.

The dismal thoughts had her sighing out loud and Wyatt glanced over at her.

"Chloe, I think I can count on one hand the times I've seen you smile this past week."

"I'm sorry I'm such bad company, Wyatt. But remember, I asked you to stay home."

"Hellfire, I'm not complaining about your company! I don't like to see you so worried."

Shaking her head, she lifted her eyes to the roof of the car. "Wyatt, you can't understand what I'm feeling. You've never had to…wonder where your next dollar was coming from. I need at least fifty tons of cattle and horse feed delivered to the ranch. The feed mill won't bring it until I pay them what I already owe them. And that's only a part of what the ranch needs." She looked over at him. "I'm sure you're wondering why I don't sell some of the cattle or horses?"

He nodded, and she turned her grim gaze back out the windshield. "I suppose if I'm turned down today, I'll have to. But once the livestock is gone, there won't be much of a ranch left. There won't be anything to build on. It'll just be a bunch of empty land and stables and barns. "I can't…bear to think of it that way."

As Wyatt listened to her, he knew a lesser woman would have already broken long ago from the strain. And he thought of the women in the past who had asked him for money. They had made their needs sound so desperate to him at the time. But now looking back, he was struck by how frivolous their wants had been. A car. A trip to Mexico. A piece of jewelry for investment. Stock in a new company that was sure to make a fortune. He'd been a gullible soft touch back then and because he'd been used, he had turned, almost drastically, the other way. If anyone even mentioned the word money to him now, he resented it.

"Have you already borrowed from the bank?"

Her expression grim, Chloe nodded. "It was absolutely necessary. A drought was on and we had to start feeding early and then Belinda torched most of our best pasture range..." She broke off, covering her mouth with her hand as she realized what she was saying. Wyatt couldn't help what his sister had done. And she didn't want to hurt him anymore by bringing it up. When she had decided that, she didn't know. She only knew that he'd become far more than just Belinda's brother to her. "I'm sorry, Wyatt. I'm not trying to persecute your sister. For a long time I wanted to. Even when you first arrived I was carrying some pretty heavy stuff around about her. But..." She glanced at his dark profile. "I don't want to hurt you, Wyatt. I know you must have loved her."

She'd said a lot of things to him, but none of them had left him feeling so open, so vulnerable, so very much in love with her.

"I did love my sister. But I'm not blind or a fool, Chloe. I can see how she damaged your family. Harlan told me about the fire and how he and Rose were nearly killed. I'm just thankful there wasn't a second tragedy to this story."

Chloe couldn't help it, she reached over and touched his forearm. "Thank you, Wyatt."

Chloe needed all sorts of things. Feed for her livestock, firewood to heat her house, groceries for the cupboards that were growing barer with each passing day. She needed basic, essential things. Yet all she really wanted or asked from him was understanding. The whole idea overwhelmed him with emotion.

They were entering the edge of Ruidoso Downs when he finally spoke. "Chloe, if you need money there's really no need for you to try to take out a second mortgage. I can lend it to you."

He knew better than to say give. He knew she wouldn't go for that. Lend sounded more impersonal and that's the way she seemed to want things between them. Until he kissed her. But he couldn't let himself think about kissing her right now.

Her jaw dropped as she stared at him. "No way! I—I'd sell the Bar M before I took money from you!"

If Wyatt had wondered what love was really like before, he certainly knew now. Her refusal to accept his help cut like a knife in the heart. He wanted to give to her. Everything, anything he had. He wanted to make her smile, see her eyes light with happiness. If that took his money, then he was thrilled he had it to give.

"Why?"

Her mouth gaped open even wider. "Why?" she repeated. "I'll never forget the things you said to me that night in the study. You thought I wanted your money! I guess you still think I want it and for some reason you've decided you're willing to give it to me. But I don't care. I'd never take your money. I'd let the ranch sink first!"

Without a word, Wyatt wheeled his car into the nearest parking area and killed the motor. Chloe looked around to see they were in front of a roadside fruit stand that was closed for the season.

"Why are you stopping? If you don't hurry the loan officers will be gone to lunch."

Reaching across the car seat, he caught her by the shoulders and pulled her toward him. "I don't care if we are late! I want to know why you're so against accepting my help? You told me a few moments ago you didn't hold my sister's behavior against me.''

Her heart thundering in her ears, she shook her head. ''I don't. Your being Belinda's brother has nothing to do with this.''

''Then you don't like me?''

Like him? What a milk-mild word to describe how she felt about Wyatt. He was a light she carried in her heart. She thought of him through all her waking hours. She ached for him, imagined how it would be to be his wife and the woman he really loved.

''Yes. I like you. But I do have pride, Wyatt. Even if I don't have money.''

''Pride can leave you very cold and hungry.''

His face was so close to her she couldn't stop her eyes from dropping to his lips. ''I don't want to be...beholden to you. Can't you understand that?''

''No,'' he whispered, his mind reeling with the urge to kiss the red lipstick off her mouth. ''I want to help you.''

Chloe couldn't prevent her eyes from closing. ''You came here to get the twins. Not to help me.''

He groaned, his fingers tightened on her shoulders. ''This has nothing to do with the twins, Chloe! I want to help you because I love you. Isn't that a good enough reason?''

Her eyes flew open and she shoved herself away from him.

''It's no reason at all. Because you don't love me. I won't let you!''

He laughed but the sound held no humor. ''You won't *let* me? Just how do you plan to stop me?''

Huddling as close to the door as she could get, Chloe said, ''I'll be...so awful to be around, you won't be able to stand the sight of me.''

His mind working overtime, he started the car engine.

"You've already shown me you can be a shrew. You'll have to think of something else to put me off."

She stared out the window at the cold, drizzling rain. "Don't do this, Wyatt. Don't complicate things for me. I...can't bear much more."

No. Wyatt didn't expect she could hold up under any more work and worries. What's more, he didn't want her to have to.

From where Wyatt sat in the bank lobby, he could see Chloe sitting across from a loan officer not much older than herself. From his own experience in business, he knew it was the young ones who were quick simply to view a thing as black and white figures on paper, rather than sit back and consider what their decision might mean to someone's life. So he was hardly surprised when Chloe came out of the office with a low, dejected look on her face.

"No dice, huh?"

Shoving the strap of her purse up on her shoulder, she shook her head. "It would be a bad risk for the bank to invest any more money in the Bar M. Especially with cattle prices the way they are nowadays. Hellfire, the Bar M doesn't just deal in cattle! But he's so wet behind the ears he doesn't know how hard it is to come by good horse-flesh. You can't just find it anywhere, and I've got it!"

"Did you tell him that?"

She let out a disgusted breath. "I tried, but I could tell he had already made up his mind before I even got around to the horses."

Wyatt took her by the elbow and pushed her down on the small couch he'd been sitting on. "You wait here. I might have a little luck persuading him."

"No! Wyatt! He doesn't know you! And it isn't your problem!" she said, jumping up and grabbing hold of his arm before he could walk away.

He pushed her down on the couch a second time.

"Chloe, please don't pick this moment to show me your shrewish side. Wait until we get home."

Home. He was calling the Bar M home now? What did it mean? "I'm...not trying to be difficult. I just don't know what you can do."

He gave her a smile of pure male confidence. "I'm a very persuasive man when I want to be, Chloe."

For the next twenty minutes Chloe fidgeted and squirmed on the couch. What was he doing in there? What could he be saying? She didn't want him to beg for her. She wasn't going to beg anyone for money. She'd sell a horse or two and eventually if the ranch went under, then so be it. At least she would have gone down fighting.

The moment Wyatt came out of the office she rose to her feet. "Wyatt, what in the world has been going on in there? I told you—"

"He needs to see you."

"What?" She frowned at him. "I've said all I want to say to that man!"

"Chloe, he wants you back in there. To sign some papers."

Her eyes grew wide, and she gripped his upper arm. "Wyatt, what have you done?"

He shrugged and did his best to keep a straight face. "Nothing except reason with the man. I think he understands that to invest a little more money in the Bar M now will assure him of getting all his money back in the future when you've gotten things pulled together again."

Hope rushed through her, lighting her eyes like a Christmas tree. "You mean he's going to lend me the money?"

Wyatt smiled and knew deep inside he'd done the right thing. Seeing the glow of renewed hope on Chloe's face was worth every penny of it.

"I told you I was a persuasive man. Oh, and Chloe," he said as he nudged her toward the office. "I managed to squeeze three thousand more than you were asking out of him.''

Three thousand over what she'd asked for? Praise the Lord! She didn't know how Wyatt had done it, but for as long as she lived Chloe would never forget this. Raising herself up on tiptoe, she kissed his cheek. ''You're stubborn and you won't listen to a word I say,'' she whispered for his ears only. ''But thank you.''

Wyatt hadn't known love could turn such a little kiss and simple words into something so special. There was a warm happy glow in the middle of Wyatt's chest such as he had never felt before. ''You're welcome, Chloe.''

That evening Wyatt called both of Chloe's sisters and invited them over for supper. All of them had been over the night before, but he knew Chloe was excited about getting the money and wanted to share the news. He also wanted her to see how much he liked her family and wanted to be a part of them.

He knew Sandra and some of his friends back in Houston wouldn't understand him. They would probably even tell him he was crazy to involve himself with a woman who was clinging to a dying ranch, a woman who could never have children, nor would ever consider living in a metropolis like Houston. But they didn't know Chloe. She was the most real woman he'd ever known. She was brave and strong and beautiful, and he couldn't imagine leaving this place and never seeing her again. She had changed his life and he would never be able to go back to what he'd been before Chloe.

Chloe was in the bathroom giving the twins a bath when knuckles rapped against the door and Justine called out.

''Chloe, are you in there? It's me and Rose.''

Keeping one eye on the babies, she rose and opened the door. Her sisters stepped inside the small room.

"What are you doing here?" she asked.

"Wyatt called and invited us for supper, didn't you know?" Justine asked.

Rose knelt down beside the tub and began playing with Adam and Anna. "What happened to their little boat? I don't see it floating around with the rest of this stuff." She picked up a ducky and gave it a loud squeeze. The babies both laughed and splashed water all the way to the ceiling.

"Adam bit a hole in the boat, so it won't float anymore."

"Naughty boy!" Rose scolded. "Why can't you be as sweet as your sister?"

As soon as the words were out, Anna flung a floating toy straight at Rose's head. It plopped against her temple and water poured down the side of her face and onto her sweater. She laughed and motioned for Chloe to take her place.

"They're your little darlings now. I'm soaked enough for one night."

"Wyatt said you had some good news for us. What is it?" Justine asked, resting her hip against the vanity counter.

She shrugged. "The banker loaned us the money we needed. Three thousand over the amount we talked about needing last night."

Justine and Rose both squealed with surprise.

"Three thousand!" Justine exclaimed. "I can't believe it."

"How did you manage that?" Rose asked in a stunned voice. "I would have sworn you couldn't have gotten another penny."

"At first he turned me down flat. Then Wyatt went in and had a little talk with him and..." She snapped her fingers. "I got the money and more."

Rose and Justine exchanged surprised looks.

"Well," Rose said, "I'm shocked. I was already trying to decide what cattle would be best to sell."

Chloe gave them a lukewarm smile at best. "Well, you can forget about selling the cattle for now. At least for a few more months."

Justine and Rose exchanged worried glances as Chloe dipped her head and began washing Anna.

"Chloe, aren't you happy?" Rose asked.

"Sure I am."

"You don't act or look like you are," Justine reasoned. "I would have thought you'd be dancing a jig."

She lifted Anna out of the tub and stood her on a fluffy throw rug. Rose quickly wrapped the baby in a towel and began drying her hair.

"I was pretty thrilled this morning. But I guess as the day wore on reality has set in. I don't see what good this money is going to do us if we can't ever pay it back. We're only postponing the inevitable."

Justine's mouth fell open as she stared at her younger sister. "That's a bunch of nonsense. Especially coming from you. The new calf crop in the spring will get us on our feet. We might still be a little shaky, but we'll be standing."

"That's right," Rose spoke up as she snuggled Anna in her arms. "We've made it through the worst. Now is not the time to give up."

Chloe sniffed and wiped her disheveled hair back out of her eyes. "I'm trying not to, sis. But it's getting harder each day." She picked up Adam and wrapped him in a towel, then sitting down on the edge of the tub, pulled the boy onto her lap. "Mainly, I'm worried about Wyatt. I still don't know exactly what he plans to do about the twins. He's liable to want to take them any day."

Rose solemnly shook her head. "No. Since I've begun to know him, I don't believe he would do that."

"I agree," Justine added, her hands linked beneath the

mound of her soon-to-be-born baby. "He's not a spiteful man."

"But he thinks the twins deserve a richer life than I can give them. Is he right? Am I being selfish wanting them here with me?"

"Oh, Chloe, darling," Rose said as she sat down beside her on the edge of the tub and balanced Anna on her knees. "The twins are our family. And as far as I'm concerned we have a good life here. Maybe you won't be able to give them every little thing they want, but they'll be loved and sheltered."

Tears gathered in Chloe's eyes and she tried valiantly to blink them away. "I'm sorry. I don't know what's the matter with me. Ever since Wyatt came I haven't been making a bit of sense."

Rose glanced at Justine, who in turn smiled knowingly.

"Has Wyatt mentioned anymore about taking the twins back to Houston with him?" Justine asked.

Chloe's head swung back and forth. "He said…" Her eyes lifted to the ceiling as she drew in a shaky breath. "He implied the twins needed both of us. Whatever that means."

"Maybe he means something like joint custody," Justine said thoughtfully. "You have them awhile, then he takes them for a while. That might seem like the fair thing to him. But frankly I don't like the idea of the babies being dragged from one home to the other. They'd never get a sense of belonging."

"I'm not so sure that's Wyatt's meaning." Rose looked to Justine. "Wyatt told Chloe he loves her."

Chloe let out a tortured groan. Justine smiled broadly.

"Oh. So now we're getting down to the root of the matter. I thought the vibes between you two were getting pretty thick."

"Justine, I'm not in the mood for a lecture about love and marriage and all that garbage about a man not caring whether I can have babies or not. You know that isn't the case. Roy is ecstatic you've given him Charlie and now the baby that's on the way.''

Justine shook her pretty head. ''Of course he's ecstatic. But I like to think he loved me enough to marry me whether we ever had children or not.''

''Well, I can tell you for sure that Wyatt doesn't care for me that way. He's a man who has always been able to have anything he wanted. Why would he settle for less now, with me?'' She shook her head emphatically. ''No. The idea of me and Wyatt together—I want you both to get it out of your minds. I certainly have!''

In the kitchen, Harlan and Roy stood with their arms folded across their chests while they watched Wyatt grill pork chops. The two men weren't much in the way of cooks, but they had set the table and iced the glasses for tea.

''I wonder what those women are doing? They've been back in the nursery for ages,'' Harlan said.

Roy chuckled. ''When Justine gets to visiting with her sisters, she loses all track of time. We'll probably have to go after them.''

Wyatt glanced up from the sizzling skillet of meat to the two brothers-in-law. The first time he'd seen the two men together he'd noticed a close bond between them. And now, even though they treated him like a friend, he was jealous of their connection to each other and their wives.

''Can I ask you two something?''

''Sure, go ahead,'' Roy said. He reached over and pinched a bit of crust off a chop that Wyatt had already placed on a platter.

''Did you guys…have trouble persuading your wives to marry you?''

Roy looked at Harlan, and both men began to laugh.

''Trouble wouldn't exactly describe what we went

through," Harlan told him. "Roy and I both had to wage an all-out war to win our wives."

"Are you thinking about getting married, Wyatt?" Roy asked.

Wyatt glanced over the men's shoulders toward the swinging batwing doors. Still no women in sight, so he said, "Before I came out here to New Mexico, I wasn't in any big hurry to find a wife." He awkwardly cleared his throat as he pushed the sizzling meat around with a long cooking fork. "But Chloe has...well, I guess you could say she's gotten to me. I don't know how, but she has. And now I can't get to first base with her. She's like a balked mule."

Harlan nodded knowingly, while Roy chuckled and patted Wyatt on the shoulder.

"Believe me, Chloe's sisters are just as mule-headed. Isn't that right, Harlan?"

"Amen to that," Harlan agreed.

"So what did you two do? What do I need to do with Chloe? She doesn't trust me an inch, and her pride is as big as Texas."

"If she's like Rose," Harlan spoke up, "she just needs to know how much you really care about her."

"Harlan's right," Roy seconded. "That's all Justine really wanted from me. Just to know I wanted her and only her."

"But how do you tell them that and make them believe it? If it takes magic, I guess I don't have it. Because every time I open my mouth, Chloe closes her ears."

"Sometimes words just don't cut it with women," Roy said with another comforting pat to Wyatt's shoulder. "They have to be shown a thing or two."

And how did a man do that? Wyatt wondered. What could he show Chloe that he hadn't already told her? How could he ever make her see that he loved her for herself and no other reason?

Chapter Eleven

Later that night after the rest of the family had left, Wyatt and Chloe sat in the living room watching the twins have their last romp before bedtime.

For some reason Adam more than Anna had taken to Wyatt. The baby was constantly crawling up to him, tugging on his jean leg and whining for his attention. This evening was no exception. For the past ten minutes Adam had stood holding onto Wyatt's knees and threatening to cry.

"Is he wanting in my lap? Or just what is he trying to tell me?" Wyatt asked Chloe as Adam's fussing grew to loud wails.

"I warned you about carrying him around," she said to him.

Frowning at Chloe, he said, "I tried to do like you said. But I can't bear to hear him cry. And I don't want him thinking I'm mean."

Smiling wryly, Chloe rolled her eyes. She'd never seen a man pamper a baby so much in her life. And not just Adam. When Anna decided she did want Wyatt's attention, he gave it to her. About the only time he wasn't entertaining the twins was when they were both asleep.

"He knows you're a sucker for tears," Chloe told him. "That's why he turns them on."

As Wyatt looked at her his eyes narrowed and the corners of his mouth lifted. "If you know I'm a sucker for tears, why haven't you been turning them on?"

She lifted her chin. "Any woman who deliberately acts weak to get what she wants from a man is an insult to our gender. Besides," she added primly, "there's not anything I want from you."

No. She didn't want his money. She didn't want to marry him. But she did want him in the most basic, physical way. Just as he wanted her. He guessed he should be thankful for that much, at least.

Rising from the chair, Wyatt took Adam by both hands. "Okay son. We'll walk for a while. Maybe you'll like that."

The minute Wyatt began helping the boy totter across the floor, Adam let out a squeal of joy so loud Chloe and Wyatt both laughed.

"So why didn't you tell me you wanted to walk?" Wyatt asked the baby as they ventured toward the row of windows facing the yard.

Chloe smiled to herself at the sight of the tall handsome man and the tiny little boy learning his first steps. Then just as quickly, her joy faded and she was swamped with regret and sadness.

Wyatt was a great father to the twins and he would be a wonderful father to his own children someday. Chloe wished with all her heart she could be the woman to give him those children. But fate had already dealt her cards. She had to play them out alone. Or find a man who was totally opposed to having children. But in her opinion that sort of man wasn't capable of real love.

"Chloe, look! Look! Adam is walking by himself!"

His excited voice jerked her out of her deep thoughts and she looked over to see Adam taking one tentative step and then another.

"How did you make him do that?" She jumped from the couch and went over to the two of them. Kneeling down in front of Adam she stretched her arms out to him.

"Come here, darling. Show me how you can walk," she coaxed.

Squealing with the joy of motoring himself, Adam tottered toward her. His steps were shaky and he was listing to one side by the time he reached Chloe, but the awed look on his face said he knew he'd just accomplished a great feat.

Chloe grabbed him up and smothered his face with kisses. "What a wonderful boy you are, Adam!"

He giggled and cooed and Chloe tickled his belly.

Wyatt smiled at the two of them. "Who says boys are slower maturing?" Wyatt said smugly. "In this case Adam beat his sister walking."

"Well, we'll see about that. If Adam can do it, so can Anna. She just needs a little more courage." Chloe went over to where Anna stood holding onto the couch, watching the three of them with a guarded eye. Chloe took the little girl by the hand and led her out into the middle of the room.

"Okay, Anna. It's time you showed Mr. Wyatt Sanders what we women can do." Chloe continued to lead her around the open area of the room. The further they traveled, the less she balanced the little girl.

Finally she pulled her finger from Anna's grasp and the baby girl took a few tottery steps on her own, then just as quickly plopped her bottom on the floor and began to cry.

"Oh, Anna. We can't let Wyatt and Adam outdo us," Chloe pleaded with the baby. "Come on, honey. Walk. Don't be afraid."

Anna must have sensed the spotlight was on her, or

she'd already learned about the battle of the sexes. The curly-haired tot rolled to her haunches, stood straight up, then walked sturdily to Chloe's arms.

"Yeah! What a girl!" Chloe cried with joy. She swung the baby into her arms and covered her face with kisses much the same as she'd done to Adam.

As Wyatt watched, he tried to imagine the babies in his apartment in Houston. Yet he couldn't. It was beautifully furnished, but it was sterile and empty compared to this ranch house. The babies belonged here. Just as Chloe did. But where did that leave him? Without her or the twins, he was truly a man alone.

"Okay, okay. So Anna can walk, too. But Adam beat her to it by a few minutes. You've got to give him credit for that."

Chloe laughed. "Adam must be a few minutes older— that's why he walked first."

Nearly an hour passed before the babies finally wore themselves down. Wyatt insisted he could put them both to bed without Chloe's help, so she went to the kitchen and made a pot of hot chocolate.

She was carrying it into the living room when Wyatt returned from the nursery.

Eyeing the tray in her hands, he asked with surprise, "You made us something to drink?"

She placed the tray on the coffee table in front of the couch. "Hot chocolate. I like it when the weather starts turning cold like it has tonight."

He went over to the fireplace and tossed on another log. "I know you want to be saving the wood. But I promise I'll see that you have plenty of firewood."

"Maybe we should try to cut a pickup load this weekend. The five-day weather forecast is predicting more cool weather. At this rate we're going to have an early winter."

"What will we do with the twins? We can't take them out in this weather to cut firewood."

"Emily will be out of school. I'm sure she'll be more than happy to watch them."

He eased down beside Chloe on the leather couch. "Emily is a sweet young woman. I'm afraid to think how a daughter of mine would turn out if I had to raise her alone for seven years like Harlan did," he said.

She handed him a cup of hot chocolate and as he leaned nearer to take it, her heart thumped erratically. She couldn't deny that she wanted him close to her. But she also knew being this close to Wyatt was worse than sitting next to a sidewinder. Their bite was poisonous, but at least you could go to a doctor and get an antidote. There wasn't a cure for what Wyatt was doing to her thinking and her heart.

"You say that, but then you want to raise the twins on your own," she said pointedly.

With a tired grimace, Wyatt closed his eyes and pinched the bridge of his nose. "Back in Houston I thought I did. I thought there wouldn't be anything to it. I could hire a nanny round the clock if need be, so I wouldn't necessarily have to be tied down. And the babies would be given the best of care, anything my money could buy them." He opened his eyes and looked at her. "But since I've been staying here on the ranch, I've learned a lot of things."

Chloe studied his face for a moment, then dropped her eyes to the cup of chocolate in her hands. "You've learned how to diaper and feed a baby. How to give them a bath." She glanced at him and smiled. "And definitely how to spoil them."

His smile was sheepish. "I guess I'm better at the spoiling than anything."

Chloe placed her cup on the coffee table and went over to a small rolltop desk at the other end of the room. She pulled a padded book out of the top drawer and carried it back to the couch.

"What is that? A picture album?"

With a shake of her head, Chloe sat back down beside him. "No. It's a baby book for the twins. I've been writing down things about them since they came to the ranch. Tonight will be a big notation. They both walked alone for the first time."

She opened the book on her lap, then scooted it to her right so that he could see the pages with her.

There were all sorts of pictures with descriptions written beneath them. Several had been snapped at Justine's and Rose's weddings. Everyone was dressed up and laughing and smiling and kissing. On one page a lock of each baby's hair had been taped beneath their respective photos. Wyatt knew each comment and snapshot had been placed there with pride and love. And as she slowly flipped the pages and pointed things out to him, he felt a lump growing bigger and bigger in his throat.

"This is—something to be cherished," he said huskily.

"I wanted to be able to look back and...remember." She closed the book and clutched it against her bosom. If he took the twins, it might be all she ever had of them. The thought was so crushing, her eyes very nearly filled with tears.

"Chloe, I..." He took the book and laid it on the coffee table, then caught her chin and turned her face to his. "I want to talk to you about something."

Her breath caught in her throat as she looked into his eyes. What was he going to say now? How could she keep on fighting him when the warmth from his eyes was touching her heart, filling it with love?

"Wyatt, before you say anything I...want to thank you for cooking and inviting my family over tonight. It meant a lot to them and me."

A little smile lifted the corners of his mouth. "Don't you know by now I enjoy being around your family, too?"

Her eyes dropped to her lap. "When you first came to the ranch, I said some awful things to you. About—you not having a family or understanding what it meant to be a part of a family. I'm sorry about that, Wyatt. I should have never said it.''

''You shouldn't feel bad about that. You were scared of me. And besides, you were speaking the truth. I didn't understand what family unity really meant. I thought you were crazy when you insisted the twins would know the difference between a nanny and a family member. But I realize now what you were trying to tell me.''

With eyes full of disbelief, she studied his face. ''You do?''

Nodding, he captured both her hands in his.

''But you want the twins and—''

''Of course I want the twins,'' he interrupted. ''They're my niece and nephew, the only family I have left. And I don't think I need to tell you how much I've come to love them.''

For a while Chloe had tried to make herself believe Wyatt was nothing but a heartless, material man. An oilman who cared only about making more money. But seeing him day after day with the twins had shown her she was wrong about him. He did love the babies. And she feared he loved her, too.

''I can see that you love them,'' she said softly.

''I do. But I don't want to take them away from you. The twins belong here on the ranch. Just as you first tried to tell me.''

Her heart began to beat so hard and so fast she began to shake. ''You mean...you won't try to take them away from me? You won't go to court—''

''Court? I would have never taken you to court! I seriously doubt I would have had a leg to stand on anyway.''

Her whole inside sagged with such relief, she thought she was going to wilt. ''Wyatt, don't tell me that. You have plenty of money. It wouldn't be a problem for you to legally fight me for the twins. Like you said, you can provide them with all sorts of security. I can't.''

His expression gentle, he touched his fingers to her cheek.

''Yeah, financial security. But is that all a person really needs?'' He shook his head. ''I used to think so. But not now.''

She didn't know what to say. What to think. The twins were hers! They would always be hers.

''I...don't...'' She paused and shook her head. ''Are you being honest with me?''

He groaned at the worried disbelief on her face. ''Cross my heart.''

''You really have one of those, too?''

He chuckled softly, then pulling her into his arms, he rested his cheek against hers. ''Oh, Chloe, why did it take so long for me to finally find you?''

Her senses reeling, she buried her face against his neck and clung to him. ''Wyatt, I know you think you care for me, but—''

''I don't just care for you, Chloe. I love you.'' Taking her face between his hands, he eased her head back and looked into her eyes. ''I want to marry you.''

Her breath lodged in her throat. ''Marry? You can't be serious!''

His smile was gentle. ''I've never proposed to a woman before. Believe me, I'd have to be serious to be doing it now.''

She tried to pull out of his arms, but he held her fast.

''Wyatt, I've already told you how I feel about marriage. I'm never going to marry.''

''That's what you think.''

''That's what I know.'' Her heart beating out of control, she squirmed out of his grasp and jumped up from the couch. ''I don't want to hear any more about this love or marriage stuff.''

"Why?"

He got to his feet and started toward her. Chloe backed all the way across the room until she was at the windows and could go no farther.

"Why?" she asked inanely. "You know why. Do I have to go into it all over again?"

"If you're talking about the baby thing, then forget it. We have two babies. That's enough for me."

Her mouth fell open as another thought struck her like a bolt of lightning. "That's why...that's what this proposal is all about, isn't it? You think marrying me will be a way for you to get the twins!"

"Oh, dammit, Chloe. You're talking crazy!"

"Dammit, nothing," she hissed as he took hold of her arms. "You and I both know I'm not what you want! It's the babies! It always was!"

If he didn't love her so much he would have been furious. As it was, his heart was aching at the suspicious doubt on her face. She'd been hurt. So very hurt. But he shouldn't have to pay for another man's mistake.

"I've already told you the babies will always be yours. If it will make you feel better, I'll sign a legal document saying so."

"But there wouldn't be any point, would there be, if you and I were married?"

"No, but—"

"See. This is nothing but an easy arrangement for you!"

Helpless anger shot through him, and he gave her a little shake. "God help me, nothing about loving you has been easy, Chloe! You've fought me every step of the way. And I think it's about time you quit!"

Before she could fling another word back at him, Wyatt was kissing her. His mouth was searching and demanding, turning her whole body into a heated torch. She tried to resist him, tried to send her mind to a place faraway from his arms, but she could do neither. Whether she trusted him or not, she loved him utterly. To touch him like this was pure heaven.

"Wyatt, oh, Wyatt," she said with a groan as his teeth nibbled on her earlobe. "You don't understand what you're doing to me."

"Oh, yes, I do," he whispered as his fingers found the buttons on her flannel shirt. "Because you're doing the same thing to me."

"I couldn't be. You…you're scaring me."

His fingers stilled between her breasts. His head reared back far enough to look at her. "Scaring you? Oh, Chloe, don't you know I would never hurt you?" His eyes widened as another thought struck him. "Haven't you ever…" He reached out and touched her cheek. "Have you never had a lover?"

Chloe's eyes dropped to where his shirt opened at the neck. Black hair peeked through the edges of the material, and Chloe's fingers itched to touch him there, to push aside his shirt and run her hands across his chest.

"No. Richard spoiled my appetite for a man. Besides, I'd never have casual sex. I'm just not made for it."

Her admission both stunned and thrilled him.

"I didn't know. I didn't realize there were actually women who waited until marriage anymore."

Her face flaming, she turned her gaze to a spot across the room. "You must really be thinking I'm a freak now. A virgin and sterile to boot."

"Chloe!"

She refused to look at him. He caught her face and turned it to his. Moisture glistened in her eyes, and Wyatt knew in that moment he would never love anyone as he did Chloe. His heart was bursting to comfort her, love her, fill her with passion.

"I wish you wouldn't degrade yourself that way. I think you're beautiful and wonderful."

Her hands covered her face as tears slipped down her cheeks. "Right now you do. But that wouldn't last long."

"Tell me why."

She sniffed and wiped her eyes with the back of her hands. "I told you a moment ago you were scaring me. I wasn't talking about the idea of making love to you. You scare me when you start trying to change my thinking, my planning, my whole way of life. I've had everything settled in my mind for three or more years now. Ever since Richard opened my eyes."

He lifted his face to the ceiling and muttered something under his breath. "Just tell me where the bastard lives, Chloe! I think I'm going to go bash his head in!"

"Why? For being honest with me?"

"No! For hurting you. For being selfish and an insult to the male gender."

She walked over to the fireplace. The pine was crackling and throwing off heat, but she'd never felt so cold in her life.

"Wyatt, can you see it's not just about my inability to have children?" she asked him, then not waiting for him to answer, she went on. "We're from opposite sides of the track, Wyatt. You haven't mentioned living here, but God knows if you did, you'd probably go stark raving mad before two months were out."

"I'll go mad if I have to go back to Houston without you."

"You know I couldn't live in Houston. This is where all my family is. It's my home, a legacy from my parents. That's why I'm fighting so hard to keep it."

"I wouldn't dream of asking you to leave the Bar M."

"Then you're telling me you could live here?"

"I guess you can't believe I've come to appreciate the place."

No. She couldn't believe it. Especially when she remembered how when he'd first arrived, he viewed the place as little more than a dump.

"Actually, I can't," she said, then sighed, hoping it would help the pain in her chest go away. "Wyatt, your work is in Houston. You're a man who is accustomed to wheeling and dealing."

He opened his mouth to argue, but Chloe held up a hand. "I realize your office is able to manage without you for a few weeks. But before too long you're going to be needed there."

"And I'm not needed here. Is that what you're trying to tell me?"

The pain on his face was so real, Chloe could do nothing but go to him, fling her arms around him and bury her face against his shoulder. "Of course I need you. The twins need you. I love you. Surely you know that by now."

He didn't. But it was like being given a slice of heaven to hear it now.

"Then why are you arguing with me, Chloe?" His arms circled around her, held her trembling body tight against his.

"Because this is all wrong. It would never work. And I don't want to go through the agony of having you and then losing you."

He eased her head back and kissed her desperately. "And I don't want to go through the agony of never having you," he mouthed against her cheek. "Of never knowing how wonderful our life together could be."

Maybe it would be wonderful for a while. But how would he feel when he began to see the children of Roy and Justine, and Harlan and Rose, who already had a suspicion she might be pregnant. He would feel cheated. And eventually he would begin to blame her. Maybe not consciously, but the feeling would be there just the same.

Chloe couldn't stand that. She couldn't bear cheating him out of life's greatest gift. She loved him too much.

Perhaps one day he would realize what she was giving him now and thank her for it.

Even though there were tears on her face, she looked into his eyes and smiled. "One day you'll find someone who will make you happy, Wyatt. She'll give you love and children and she'll know how to live around moneyed people. She won't wear boots and spurs and have horse hair sticking to the seat of her pants."

"Is that what you think will make me happy? If it is, you don't know me at all."

The tearful smile on her face was the saddest thing Wyatt had ever seen. "No. It's you who don't know yourself."

Hoping his lips could persuade where his words could not, he bent his head and kissed her. She closed her eyes, held herself to him, tasted the love on his lips until her heart could stand no more. Then with a muffled sob, she slipped from his arms and ran to her room.

For the next two days the weather stayed abnormally cool, but dry. Chloe was able to throw herself into her work and stay out of the house as much as possible.

Wyatt knew she was deliberately avoiding him, but he didn't try to push himself on her. He could see she was in mental agony over all that he'd told her, and he figured the most he could do was give her time to sort it all out in her mind.

But how much time he had left here on the ranch was something he was no longer sure about. Kitty had unexpectedly returned home this morning and although the older woman still had a walking cast, she was able to maneuver herself around the house pretty well. Kitty seemed eager and, if not completely ready, then partially able to take over her job again.

Wyatt had never felt so useless or unwanted in his life, and he knew he couldn't continue to mope around this place waiting for Chloe to figure out the two of them should be married. He had to do something to wake her up.

He found Kitty at the kitchen table playing solitaire with a dog-eared deck of cards. He pointed out a play to her, then asked, "Do you think you could manage the twins for awhile?"

"Sure. If they wake up and start running all over the house, I'll put them in their playpen."

He gave her a grateful wink. "I think I'll go down to the stable and see if I can be any help to Chloe."

The older woman's brows lifted with surprise. "You think she'll let you help her? She's been awfully testy that I can see."

Wyatt reached for a jacket hanging on a peg near the back door. "She's mad because I asked her to marry me."

Kitty didn't seem a bit surprised. In fact, she chuckled and said, "Then you'd better make her glad."

"And how does anyone make Chloe glad? I've never seen a more bull-headed woman."

Kitty nodded. "Yep. She gets that from her daddy. Once Tomas made up his mind about something it was hell to change it."

"Well, I'm going to try my best to change Chloe's," he said, then walked a few steps back over to Kitty. "How would you feel about having me around her permanently?"

A sly smile on her face, Kitty waved Wyatt toward the door. "Go do what you can do with Chloe. I don't want to lose a good cooking partner."

The afternoon sky was overcast, the wind cold and sharp as Wyatt walked to the stable. Yesterday Rose and Harlan had penned several head of cattle to vaccinate and dehorn them. But the two of them had finished the work early this morning and the pens were now empty, except for Martin, the orphaned calf.

He found Chloe cleaning out a horse stall at the end of the stable. Her flannel shirt was rolled above her elbows and her face grimaced with strain as she tossed a shovel of dirty hay and wood shavings into the wheelbarrow.

"How about letting me do that for a while?"

She looked up to see Wyatt standing at the open door of the stall. He was wearing an old denim jacket and a pair of cotton work gloves. Her heart ached at the sight of him.

"I'm doing okay." She bent to scoop up another shovel full.

"Give me the shovel and sit down for a while."

"I said I'm doing okay. Who's taking care of the twins?"

"They're both asleep. Kitty says she can manage without me for a while."

Chloe frowned. "Her leg is in a cast. How do you think she can run down two babies who've just found their legs and want to run all over the house?"

Wyatt knew it wasn't the babies or Kitty she was really concerned about, it was herself. She didn't want to face him, or her feelings. But that was too bad. He'd tried to be gentle, he'd tried to give her time to think. He'd tried to love her. It was time she dealt with him.

He folded his arms across his chest. "I came down here to help you. And don't try to tell me you don't need it," he added as she opened her mouth to butt in. "I haven't forgotten you told me you once had five wranglers around here to work the place. You and I only make up for two."

She continued to dig to the bottom of the dirty stall. "Rose is over in the cattle barn."

"So that makes three. We're still short."

Seeing he wasn't going anywhere, she tossed the shovel onto the wheelbarrow and planted her hands on her hips.

"You're deliberately trying to make me angry, aren't you?"

He smiled because he couldn't help it. She looked so beautiful when her green eyes snapped and her cheeks flamed as red as her hair.

"I don't have to try to make you angry, Chloe. You seem to manage to get that way all by yourself."

She felt awful. But dammit, she was about to crack and he knew it! She'd had so many worries, so many problems to deal with. And now she'd fallen in love with a man she couldn't marry. He knew how she felt about him. Was he down here trying to rub salt in her wounds? Why couldn't he go on and let her hurt in peace?

"I'm sorry, Wyatt. I do appreciate your offer. But I think it would be better if you went back...to the house."

He stepped into the stall with her, and Chloe's heart nearly stopped altogether. If he touched her now, she didn't know what she would do.

"Were you going to say Houston?"

The thought had crossed Chloe's mind. Both of them would be better off once he was gone. He could find someone else and she could...well, she could try to forget.

"Kitty is back. And I'm sure if you really thought about it, you'd realize you're ready to go."

He frowned at her. "Have you always tried to tell other people what to do, what they're thinking?"

"I don't try to tell people what they're thinking! That's crazy!"

"You're right. It is, so why are you?"

She drew in a bracing breath. "Because you're different, you don't seem to know your own mind."

He laughed. "So you have to tell me, huh? Well, I've got a newsflash for you, Chloe. I do know my own mind, and what's more you're wasting your time and mine by trying to change it."

The steely-eyed look on his face set her heart to a throbbing gallop. In an unconscious act of defense, she picked up the shovel and jabbed it in the ground in front of her.

"What do you mean?"

He stepped up to her, took the shovel handle from her hands and tossed the tool in the corner out of the way.

"I'm not going back to Houston, Chloe. That's final. I'm staying here, and we're getting married. Like two normal people in love."

Her mouth fell open. "You can't just…refuse to leave!"

"I just have. What's more, Kitty doesn't want me to go. And I don't think the rest of your family does either."

He was right about that. None of her family wanted Wyatt to leave. They all liked him and thought he should stay here close to the twins. But Chloe was the one living with him! And that had to stop! It had to! Before she lost control and gave in to him.

Groaning deep in her throat, she turned her back to him. "What did I do to deserve this? Why are you deliberately trying to make things…so hard for me?"

The agony in her voice ripped at Wyatt's heart. Stepping closer, he put his hands on the back of her slender shoulders. "Chloe, I love you so much. Don't you know that when you hurt, I hurt?"

Her head bent. "I wish…you didn't love me," she said, her voice low and choked.

"Then you do believe me? You don't think I want to marry you just for the twins?"

Chloe had lain awake for hours last night, weighing every word, every kiss, every touch he'd ever given her. And she couldn't doubt his love.

"No."

The one word came out in a painful whisper. Wyatt's hands tightened on her shoulders. His head dipped and he nuzzled his nose against the side of her silky hair.

Chloe closed her eyes and for a moment considered throwing every damn care and caution to the wind. She wanted him so badly, loved him so much. Why not be selfish and keep him? Why not, for once in her life think of her own wants and needs? But she couldn't. It just wasn't in her to hurt him that way.

"Oh, Wyatt, don't you see that I don't want you to love me? It only makes it that much harder for me to give you up."

He whirled her round and his eyes met and pleaded with hers. "You're not giving me up! I told you—"

"I don't care what you told me. I'm not going to marry you and ruin your life."

Ruin his life? What did she think she was doing to it now?

His eyes suddenly glittering, Wyatt said, "I came down here to work. And maybe talk. I didn't come down here for this. But by God, since you asked for it—"

The next thing Chloe knew she was crushed in his arms, his mouth devouring hers.

She squirmed against him, then wilted as a rush of sweet desire poured through every inch of her. It wasn't fair that she wanted him this much, that she ached for him to hold her and never let her go.

"You're not going to give me up! Or this up! So get used to it," he ordered against the soft curve of her lips.

The idea there was no place to run, or hide, or escape from him, sent desperation clawing at her insides. She couldn't hold up to this! How could she keep on fighting him?

With a choked sob, she tore out of his arms and ran from the stable. Outside, her pony horse, Pablo, was tethered to a hitching post. Chloe grabbed up the reins and leapt into the saddle. By the time Wyatt ran out the door after her, she was galloping away as if a fire were at her heels.

"Dammit all!" He kicked the dirt with frustration, then glanced around him. What in hell was he going to do now?

The sight of her was growing to a small speck on the

western range as Wyatt turned on his heel and headed toward the cattle barn.

Moments later Rose looked up as he entered the dusty dim building. She was spreading alfalfa in a long, low manger. The pungent smell filled his nostrils as he approached Chloe's older sister.

"Wyatt, what are you doing down here? Is something wrong?"

He supposed Rose could tell by the look on his face that all was not well with him.

"Actually, yes. Chloe is…well, she's upset. And I've got to go after her."

"After her. Where did she go? I thought she was cleaning out the stable?"

"She was. Until I showed up to help her. We had a row, and she took off on a horse hell-bent for leather. That woman's name should have been rawhide instead of Chloe!"

Rose's face remained calm as she continued to spread hay. "What color was the horse?"

"What?" Wyatt was itching to race after her and Rose wanted to talk about the horse?

"The color of the horse Chloe rode off on. Was it sorrel? 'Cause it sure as heck better not have been Pie. I'll get her good if she cripples him in a rabbit hole."

"No. The horse wasn't red. At least I don't think so. It was dark. Like brown or black. I don't know what horses' colors are called."

"Was it dark red with a black mane and tail and stockings?"

"Yes!" Maybe now he could make progress.

"That's Pablo, the horse she uses to pony her racehorse stock. You might be able to catch him if you ride flat out. Then, too, Chloe might cool down and pull up before long. Either way, you really shouldn't worry about her."

"But I am worried, Rose. She was very upset. We...we've been fighting about getting married. She has this damn notion she can't be my wife because she's unable to have children."

Rose dropped the last block of hay into the manger and looked at him. "She told you about her condition? How Richard dropped her after he'd already asked her to marry him?"

Grim faced, Wyatt nodded. "It doesn't matter about any of that, Rose. I've tried to tell her that she and the twins are all I need, but she refuses to listen."

"She's afraid, Wyatt," Rose said simply. "She's afraid you'll say it's enough right now. Then later it won't be. And losing you like that would be far worse for her."

Wyatt let out a heavy breath. "Is that what you think I'd do?"

"No," Rose answered. "But Chloe probably does. She's always vowed she will never marry. She thinks she's unworthy of being a wife."

"She's so wrong."

Rose nodded. "I know. And I guess it didn't help matters this morning when I told her I was pregnant."

Wyatt was happy for Rose. She and Harlan deserved another child together. Just as Justine and Roy did. But oh, God, how empty and left out Chloe must be feeling at this moment. His heart ached for her.

"Congratulations, Rose. I'm very pleased for you and Harlan."

She smiled and patted his arm. "I know you are. Now what do you plan to do about Chloe?"

"I thought you might help me saddle a horse so I can go find her."

"Have you ever ridden before?"

His expression sheepish, he said, "Once in summer camp when I was twelve years old."

With a soft laugh, Rose motioned for him to follow her out of the barn. "I'll let you ride Pie."

"But he's *your* horse!"

"He is. But if I tell him to treat you well, he will. Chloe doesn't want a husband with a broken neck, and that's what any of those hot-blooded horses of hers would do to you."

Wyatt swallowed his sudden uneasiness. "I'll do my best not to hurt him."

Rose laughed again. "I'm sure Pie will be in good hands. You just make sure you pick out some landmarks on the way. Otherwise, if you go very far you're gonna be as lost as a goose flying south in the summer."

Wyatt glanced toward the western horizon where Chloe had disappeared. "Do you have any idea where she might have gone?"

"Which way did she go?"

"West over that ridge." He pointed in the direction he'd last seen Chloe.

"There's a windmill and water tank a couple of miles over that way. She'll probably head toward it. But she'll gather herself together after a while and come home, Wyatt. Why don't you just wait for her here?"

He shook his head vigorously and nudged Rose on toward the stable. "No. She's hurting, Rose. I don't want her out there like this. I've got to find her."

Minutes later, aboard Rose's sorrel cow horse, Wyatt headed out across the range. The feel of the horse and saddle beneath his legs felt strange and awkward. Rose had given Wyatt a five-minute riding lesson, but he wasn't sure he remembered half of it.

Keep his feet in the stirrups. Lay the reins against the side of the horse's neck to tell him which direction to go. Pull gently back on the reins to stop him. It sounded easy enough, Wyatt supposed. But Pie seemed to have the idea that walking was boring. He wanted to travel at a bone-jarring trot. If Wyatt pulled on the reins to slow him down, the horse stopped completely. When he relaxed the reins, Pie went right back to a trot.

By the time Wyatt had ridden a half a mile, he was sure his pelvis bones were permanently damaged and his teeth were shaken loose from his gums. But he dared not stop. He still hadn't caught a glimpse of Chloe and he wasn't about to give up finding her now.

You have to show her you love her. Harlan's advice ran through Wyatt's thoughts as he searched the horizon in front of him for a sign of Chloe.

How could he show her? Kisses hadn't done it. Words didn't seem to sink in with her. He'd tried to help her on the ranch in all the ways he could. He'd done his best to assure her the twins would always remain hers. What more could he do? What did she want him to do?

The answer to that question left him colder than the high desert wind blowing in his face.

For the past hour Chloe had sat on a rocky ledge watching the cattle graze in the distance and listening to the rhythmic creak of the windmill a few yards behind her. It was a lonely, but soothing sound and Chloe's heart had grown much calmer than when she'd first ridden away from the ranch. But the ache was still there in the middle of her chest, heavy and sad and refusing to go away. Chloe supposed it was something she was going to have to get used to.

Oh, Wyatt, she silently groaned. What was she going to do? How could she live with him? How could she not?

Since Richard had rejected her, she'd had her life all neatly planned out. And up until Wyatt had come along, she'd found it rather easy to live without a man. She had her work. And later, she had hoped to adopt a child of her own. Many single women did nowadays.

But then the twins had virtually been dropped from

heaven and into her lap. Then Wyatt had followed. She loved all three. And more than anything she wished Wyatt could live here with her, be her husband and a father to the twins. But in the end, she knew she would be doing wrong to marry him, to take away his chances of ever having his own family.

She was trying so hard not to hurt Wyatt. But she knew she was. Each time she pushed him away, she could see the pain on his face. And it was killing her. Cutting her to the very bone. But she was doing it for his sake. Why couldn't he see that? Why couldn't he understand that she loved him so much she wanted him to have everything?

Suddenly several yards off to her right, a slight movement in the sagebrush caught her attention. She stared hard for long moments and was about to decide she'd imagined the whole thing when out came two coyote pups. Their scrawny little legs were tottery but they managed to scamper down a small ravine. Seconds later two adult coyotes appeared. A male and female. Obviously the pups' parents.

Chloe remained very still, watching the small family, who had not yet picked up on her presence. Mother and father sniffed the air, gave each other a few loving nips and nudges, then together went down the ravine to join their little ones.

Before long, all four coyotes were out of sight once again, camouflaged by the high stand of sagebrush. Yet the animals remained in Chloe's mind. Mother, father, babies. A family for as long as they could survive in the wild. The parents would protect each other and their offspring. Fighting to their death if need be to save their loved ones.

The whole idea brought a fresh spate of tears to Chloe's eyes. She was wiping them away, telling herself to quit feeling sorry for herself when a few yards away, Pablo lifted his head from a patch of grama grass and whinnied softly.

Sensing along with the horse that someone or something was behind her, she looked over her shoulder, than gasped out loud.

It was Wyatt on Pie! Both hands were gripping the horn as he flopped from one side of the saddle to the other.

Dear heaven, how had he ridden this far! Why was he out here?

Too stunned to move from her spot, Chloe watched him dismount awkwardly, then gingerly flex his legs. His head was bare and the wind had ruffled his black hair. With both hands, he thrust it back from his forehead, then climbed the short ledge to where Chloe sat with her knees drawn up beneath her chin.

"I didn't think I'd ever find you," he said, his voice a bit winded. He sat down beside her and drew in a long breath. "Damn, this place doesn't have any oxygen."

A wan smile touched her lips. "The elevation is about seven thousand feet here. It takes people like you awhile to get used to it."

He looked at her. "People like me? You mean, green-horn city people?"

"No. I mean people who live in low elevations like Houston."

He stretched his legs and tried not to groan at the stiffness already gripping his muscles. "You're a long way from the ranch."

"Not that far," she murmured. The sight of him made her heart thud with pain and longing.

"Rose let me ride her horse."

The pride in his voice very nearly made her start crying all over again. "I guess you realize she bestowed an honor on you. She won't let anyone on that horse. Not even Harlan."

"She was afraid one of yours would break my neck." He looked away from her. "She didn't want me to come out here after you. But I told her I had to."

"Why?"

He gave her a sidelong glance and Chloe could see love all over his face. Dear God, how could she not be selfish? How could she not grab him and hold on for life?

"You know why. You were angry and hurting and I...don't want you to...I want things between us to be right."

The cold wind had given his dark skin a ruddy hue. Chloe longed to lay her gloved hand on his cheek, warm his lips with her own. She knew it had been a physical ordeal for him to ride this far. And he'd done it for her.

"Rose was right," she said, her thoughts making her voice husky. "You shouldn't have come out here. You could have fallen off and broken a bone. You could have gotten lost. Do you have any idea what it would be like out here in the dark, with the temperature dropping?"

"In other words, I was a fool for coming after you."

She couldn't look at him as tears collected in her eyes. "Reckless, maybe. But I'd never call you a fool."

His heart soared. But though he longed to reach for her, he kept his hands on his thighs.

"You know, Chloe, for the past week, I've been thinking about you and me and the twins. About us being a family. But—"

"Wyatt, please," she begged, her voice trembling. "I left the ranch because I can't take any more of this. I—"

"Chloe, just listen to me for a minute," he interrupted. She lifted moist eyes to his face and it was all Wyatt could do to keep from hauling her into his arms and burying her soft little body against him. "I'm not blind. I can see what I'm doing to you. I'm making you miserable."

Was he? Or was she making herself miserable? Chloe silently agonized.

His hand crept over and closed around hers and he was awed by its smallness, its ability to be so tough and yet so tender. But that was his Chloe. Tough and tender and oh so precious to him.

"Roy told me I needed to show you I love you. And there's only one way I can think of to do that."

Something in his face told her he was about to say something that would affect both of them for the rest of their lives.

Her fingers unconsciously tightened on his. "You don't have to show me anything, Wyatt. I know you love me. That's not the issue."

"But it is," he said softly. "I can't go on living here unless you agree to be my wife. And you can't..." He paused and drew in a painful breath. "Well, that's why I'm going back to Houston. Above anything, Chloe, I want you to be happy. And if that's what it takes, I guess there's only one thing for me to do and that's say goodbye to you and the twins."

"Goodbye?" She whispered the word as shock and loss and visions of the future tumbled through her mind.

His face grim, Wyatt nodded. "God knows it's not what I want to do, Chloe. I want to be here with you and the twins. I want us to be a family. But if that's not what you want, I realize I have to let go."

He was going to leave! There would be no more shared meals, no more laughs or groans over the twins antics. She would never see the babies cradled in his arms again. She would never feel those same arms around her. His kisses and words of love would only be a memory. How could she bear the loneliness? But she had to! Didn't she?

While the dreadful thoughts raced through her head, Wyatt rose to his feet.

He looked down at her, his gray eyes moist. "Goodbye, Chloe."

She couldn't bear the anguish on his face. She fixed her eyes on the far off peak of Sierra Blanca. The beautiful mountain jutted twelve thousand feet toward heaven and at the moment Chloe could see it was snowing there. But it felt as if the flakes of ice were landing right here, smack in the middle of her breaking heart.

"Goodbye, Wyatt."

She didn't look as he walked away. Nor did she turn her head to see him climb stiffly back into Pie's saddle. She continued to watch the white shroud of snow fall over the mountains until she was no longer seeing anything except the vision of the coyotes. Once the animal found its mate, they traveled the rest of their lives together. Nothing but death would part them.

And suddenly she knew she could not let Wyatt leave. Selfish or not, she was like the coyote. She had found her mate and she would never let him go.

Jumping to her feet, she saw him riding away, his shoulders hunched, his head bent against the cold wind. She raced down the ledge, snatched up Pablo's reins and swung into the saddle. Houston could live without Wyatt Sanders. But she couldn't.

Wyatt didn't know what hit him as the loop of the lariat settled over his head, then tightened around his arms and chest. The commotion caused Pie to come to an abrupt halt, nearly sending Wyatt tumbling over the horse's head.

"What in hell—" His head jerked around to see Chloe right behind him, a broad grin on her face.

"You're not going anywhere, cowboy!"

"Chloe?"

Recoiling the slack in her lariat, she nudged her horse up beside Pie. "You won't go, will you, Wyatt? I told you I would never call you a fool. But I'll call myself one." Leaning out of the saddle, she grabbed his face with both hands. "Oh, Wyatt, I've been so...awful. But I don't want to ever hurt you. Can you be happy with just me and the twins? Will we really be enough for you?"

Oh, God, he would gladly give up his fortune to erase the awful doubt from her face. "Chloe. Chloe, love. Don't you realize that you are more than I ever dreamed of having?''

"But I'll never be able to give you a child.''

He shook his head and smiled. "But I'll have you, Chloe. You and me. Together. Besides, I have plenty of money—''

"Wyatt, I don't want your money or anything connected to it. I know this ranch is floundering, but we'll pull it to shore somehow. I would never have you thinking I married you for money. So go give it away. Do what you want with it. Just don't try to give it to me.''

"Chloe, just hush for a minute about the money,'' he said, pressing a finger against her lips. "Have you ever seen a specialist about your sterile condition?''

Her eyes widened at his unexpected question. "Well, not exactly a specialist. You see, I had appendicitis in high school and that's when the surgeon found the problem. But I've never been to a fertility doctor. Richard dumped me so fast I didn't have a chance to check anything out. And then—'' She shrugged. "I didn't see much point in it.''

Until this very moment he didn't realize just how unworthy Chloe felt about herself. And he vowed he would spend the rest of his life showing her how special she really was.

"Well, there is a point now. That's what I was about to say. I have the money to send you to the very best specialists. They're doing all sorts of new and wonderful things to help infertile couples now. It might be that your condition isn't so hopeless after all. But if it is—'' he smiled and leaned his mouth next to hers. "I'll still have you. And you'll have me.''

A joyous sob welled up in her throat. "And we'll have the twins,'' she said.

He grinned as happiness spilled inside him like an overturned bucket of bright sunshine. "Oh, yes, the twins. The very reason we met in the first place.''

Chloe slipped the lariat up and over his head. "I guess I got you caught well enough to take this off now," she said with a mischievous giggle.

He reached for the coiled rope. "Maybe you'd better give that thing to me. I might have to rope and tie you from time to time."

Laughing, she tossed him the lariat. Wyatt slung it over the saddle horn and together they nudged their horses toward the Bar M.

After they had ridden a short distance Chloe said, "Oh, Wyatt, we're going to be so happy."

"I can't wait to show you how happy." He'd ridden out here expecting to get one final rejection. Instead Chloe had made him the happiest man on earth. He'd never be able to figure her.

She reached for his hand and squeezed it. "I can see right now I'm going to have to teach you how to ride a horse."

Her eyes were sparkling and Wyatt suddenly thought of all the things he was going to teach her, all the things they would see and do together. His life was going to be fuller than he'd ever imagined. "I'll be your devoted pupil."

"Do you know anything about cattle?" she asked teasingly.

"Only that I like to eat steak and hamburgers."

Her sidelong glance held a bit of suspicion. "Tell me something, Wyatt. What did you really say to the banker that day I borrowed the money?"

He couldn't lie to her. But damned if he wanted another argument. "Well, I..."

He chuckled and she began to laugh. And suddenly he knew that everything was going to be all right. Chloe finally understood him and accepted his love. "I signed a paper and told him to wire my bank in Houston and have seven thousand dollars transferred to your ranch account."

Chloe wasn't surprised. She realized now that he would

do anything for her. It was an incredible feeling. "Looks like I owe you a lot."

"Nothing but your love. Think you can pay up?"

She gave him a slow, promising smile. "Only for the rest of my life."

Epilogue

Chloe waved goodbye to the last of the guests, then shut the door behind her.

Across the living room Justine sagged wearily onto the couch beside Roy, who was holding their month-old daughter, Caroline.

"I've never seen such a noisy crowd. You'd have thought it was a New Year's Eve party instead of a baby christening," Justine said with a sigh.

"I guess we invited more friends than we thought," Chloe said. "But it's been a happy day. And little Caroline doesn't seem the worse for wear." She went over to Roy and bent down to kiss her new little niece's red head.

"She hasn't let out a peep," Emily spoke up, "except when the minster got a hold of her. I don't think she liked getting water on her head."

Everyone laughed just as Rose entered the living room carrying a tray of soft drinks.

"Do I look funny or something?" she asked, glancing from one face to the next.

Harlan got up from an armchair to help his wife. "No,

Rosie, you look beautiful.'' He patted her small but protruding stomach. ''We were just laughing about little Caroline.''

He began to pass the drinks around to the rest of the family. ''Where's Wyatt?'' he asked.

''I saw him heading down the hallway a moment ago,'' Roy answered. ''Maybe he was going to go check on the twins.''

''Or wake them up so he can play with them,'' Rose said with a laugh.

''I wish Uncle Wyatt would wake the twins up!'' Charlie exclaimed. ''They're funny! Especially when Aunt Chloe has to chase after them.''

Chloe tweaked her nephew's nose. ''You would think that, little buddy.''

''Here he is,'' Justine announced as Wyatt entered the living room.

Walking over to her husband, Chloe slipped her arm through his. ''Been in the nursery trying to wake the twins?'' she teased.

Chuckling, he kissed his wife's cheek, then led her over to an empty armchair. Once she was settled, he took a seat on the floor at her feet.

It was then Chloe noticed he had a small padded book of some sort in his hand. ''What is that, honey? Something to do with your new office?''

For the past three weeks, Wyatt had been putting his own oil drilling company together. And even though most of the actual drilling would take place in northern New Mexico, he could easily direct operations from an office in Ruidoso. Chloe was very excited for him and had been helping him furnish the building with a western flair. She had also taken a trip to see a gynecologist in Albuquerque and so far the doctor had given her an encouraging diagnosis. A new laser surgery could very well make it possible for her to become pregnant and safely deliver a baby. The wonderful news had only added to Wyatt and Chloe's newfound happiness.

Wyatt answered, "No. It's nothing to do with business. You remember Belinda's landlady in Albuquerque sent some of her belongings to my office in Houston?" Chloe nodded and he went on. "Well, I had them shipped up here with a few of my trunks and last night as I was going through one of them, I found a journal."

"A journal? Of Belinda's?" Chloe leaned forward in her seat and peered at the book he was holding.

Wyatt nodded.

"Have you read it?" Roy asked.

"Most of it."

"Why didn't you say something earlier?" Kitty asked from a chair across the room.

The whole family looked at him and waited.

"I didn't want anything to spoil Caroline's christening party," he told them.

"Why? Does it say something bad that we might not want to hear? Is it about Daddy?" Chloe prodded him.

"It's all about your father," he answered. "I don't think my sister really started to live until she met him. But she didn't know how to hold on to a good thing." He opened the book, then glanced at the rest of the family circled around the room. "Do you want to hear it?"

They all agreed that they did and Wyatt began to read. A long time later after he'd read the last entry, he glanced up at his wife. There were tears on her face and he gently squeezed her knee.

"Poor Belinda," Chloe murmured. "She loved Daddy very much. But he was afraid to tell us about her and the twins. He was afraid we would never forgive him for being unfaithful to Mother."

"Well, I forgave him long ago," Rose said. "I think Belinda was right when she wrote that Tomas turned to her out of grief. He was watching Mother wither away right before his eyes. That couldn't have been easy for him."

Justine nodded in agreement. "We all know he loved Mother. When he met Belinda at the racetrack in Ruidoso, her attention must have helped him forget he was losing his wife of thirty years."

Wyatt sighed. "Well, I was relieved to read that Tomas was willingly sending the money to Belinda to support her and the babies. Like Chloe, I was afraid that maybe she had been blackmailing him."

Roy glanced lovingly down at his new daughter, then said, "I guess it wasn't until after Tomas died that she turned to drugs and alcohol."

Wyatt nodded. "She had no way of knowing he'd died suddenly of a heart attack. She thought he'd simply deserted her and the twins. I guess the loss was more than she could bear. You can tell in the latter entries she wrote that everything was becoming confused in her mind."

"She must have used all the money Tomas sent her to buy drugs," Kitty commented. "The poor girl must have been deranged with grief."

"I doubt she realized what she was doing when she tried to burn the ranch," Harlan spoke up. "I'm just sorry she had to die so young."

Chloe pressed her cheek against her husband's. "We're all sorry, darling."

"So am I," he agreed. "And sorry, too, that Tomas died before I ever had the chance to meet him."

"Their affair was tragically wrong," Chloe told him, "but you have to admit some good came out of it. They gave us the twins, and they brought us together."

His wife was right, Wyatt thought as he looked around the room at his brothers- and sisters-in-law, his nieces and nephew, and Aunt Kitty. Belinda and Tomas had brought all of them together. And he, like the rest of the family, was very grateful for that.

His heart full, he closed the journal.

* * * * *

**AVAILABLE THIS
MONTH FROM
SILHOUETTE
ROMANCE®**

MILLION DOLLAR SWEEPSTAKES
OFFICIAL RULES
NO PURCHASE NECESSARY TO ENTER

1. To enter, follow the directions published. Method of entry may vary. For eligibility, entries must be received no later than March 31, 1998. No liability is assumed for printing errors, lost, late, non-delivered or misdirected entries.

   To determine winners, the sweepstakes numbers assigned to submitted entries will be compared against a list of randomly, preselected prize winning numbers. In the event all prizes are not claimed via the return of prize winning numbers, random drawings will be held from among all other entries received to award unclaimed prizes.

2. Prize winners will be determined no later than June 30, 1998. Selection of winning numbers and random drawings are under the supervision of D. L. Blair, Inc., an independent judging organization whose decisions are final. Limit: one prize to a family or organization. No substitution will be made for any prize, except as offered. Taxes and duties on all prizes are the sole responsibility of winners. Winners will be notified by mail. Odds of winning are determined by the number of eligible entries distributed and received.

3. Sweepstakes open to residents of the U.S. (except Puerto Rico), Canada and Europe who are 18 years of age or older, except employees and immediate family members of Torstar Corp., D. L. Blair, Inc., their affiliates, subsidiaries, and all other agencies, entities, and persons connected with the use, marketing or conduct of this sweepstakes. All applicable laws and regulations apply. Sweepstakes offer void wherever prohibited by law. Any litigation within the province of Quebec respecting the conduct and awarding of a prize in this sweepstakes must be submitted to the Régie des alcools, des courses et des jeux. In order to win a prize, residents of Canada will be required to correctly answer a time-limited arithmetical skill-testing question to be administered by mail.

4. Winners of major prizes (Grand through Fourth) will be obligated to sign and return an Affidavit of Eligibility and Release of Liability within 30 days of notification. In the event of non-compliance within this time period or if a prize is returned as undeliverable, D. L. Blair, Inc. may at its sole discretion, award that prize to an alternate winner. By acceptance of their prize, winners consent to use of their names, photographs or other likeness for purposes of advertising, trade and promotion on behalf of Torstar Corp., its affiliates and subsidiaries, without further compensation unless prohibited by law. Torstar Corp. and D. L. Blair, Inc., their affiliates and subsidiaries are not responsible for errors in printing of sweepstakes and prize winning numbers. In the event a duplication of a prize winning number occurs, a random drawing will be held from among all entries received with that prize winning number to award that prize.

5. This sweepstakes is presented by Torstar Corp., its subsidiaries and affiliates in conjunction with book, merchandise and/or product offerings. The number of prizes to be awarded and their value are as follows: Grand Prize — $1,000,000 (payable at $33,333.33 a year for 30 years); First Prize — $50,000; Second Prize — $10,000; Third Prize — $5,000; 3 Fourth Prizes — $1,000 each; 10 Fifth Prizes — $250 each; 1,000 Sixth Prizes — $10 each. Values of all prizes are in U.S. currency. Prizes in each level will be presented in different creative executions, including various currencies, vehicles, merchandise and travel. Any presentation of a prize level in a currency other than U.S. currency represents an approximate equivalent to the U.S. currency value for that level, at that time. Prize winners will have the opportunity of selecting any prize offered for that level; however, the actual non U.S. currency equivalent prize if offered and selected, shall be awarded at the exchange rate existing at 3:00 P.M. New York time on March 31, 1998. A travel prize option, if offered and selected by winner, must be completed within 12 months of selection and is subject to: traveling companion(s) completing and returning of a Release of Liability prior to travel; and hotel and flight accommodations availability. For a current list of all prize options offered within prize levels, send a self-addressed, stamped envelope (WA residents need not affix postage) to: MILLION DOLLAR SWEEPSTAKES Prize Options, P.O. Box 4456, Blair, NE 68009-4456, USA.

6. For a list of prize winners (available after July 31, 1998) send a separate, stamped, self-addressed envelope to: MILLION DOLLAR SWEEPSTAKES Winners, P.O. Box 4459, Blair, NE 68009-4459, USA.

As seen on TV!
Free Gift Offer

With a Free Gift proof-of-purchase from any Silhouette® book,
you can receive a beautiful cubic zirconia pendant.

This gorgeous marquise-shaped stone is a genuine cubic
zirconia—accented by an 18" gold tone necklace.
(Approximate retail value $19.95)

Send for yours today…
compliments of ▼ *Silhouette*®

To receive your free gift, a cubic zirconia pendant, send us one original proof-of-
purchase, photocopies not accepted, from the back of any Silhouette Romance™,
Silhouette Desire®, Silhouette Special Edition®, Silhouette Intimate Moments®
or Silhouette Yours Truly™ title available in February, March and April at your favorite
retail outlet, together with the Free Gift Certificate, plus a check or money order for
$1.65 U.S./$2.15 CAN. (do not send cash) to cover postage and handling, payable
to Silhouette Free Gift Offer. We will send you the specified gift. Allow 6 to 8 weeks for
delivery. Offer good until April 30, 1997 or while quantities last. Offer valid in the
U.S. and Canada only.

Free Gift Certificate

Name: _____

Address: _____

City: _____ State/Province: _____ Zip/Postal Code: _____

Mail this certificate, one proof-of-purchase and a check or money order for postage
and handling to: SILHOUETTE FREE GIFT OFFER 1997. In the U.S.: 3010 Walden
Avenue, P.O. Box 9077, Buffalo NY 14269-9077. In Canada: P.O. Box 613, Fort Erie,
Ontario L2Z 5X3.

FREE GIFT OFFER
ONE PROOF-OF-PURCHASE

084-KFD

To collect your fabulous FREE GIFT, a cubic zirconia pendant, you must include this
original proof-of-purchase for each gift with the properly completed Free Gift Certificate.

084-KFD

**This summer, the legend
continues in Jacobsville**

A LONG, TALL
TEXAN SUMMER

Three **BRAND-NEW** short stories

This summer, Silhouette brings readers a special
collection for Diana Palmer's LONG, TALL TEXANS
fans. Diana has rounded up three **BRAND-NEW**
stories of love Texas-style, all set in Jacobsville,
Texas. Featuring the men you've grown to love from
this wonderful town, this collection is a must-have
for all fans!

*They grow 'em tall in the saddle in Texas—and
they've got love and marriage on their minds!*

Don't miss this collection of original Long, Tall Texans
stories…available in June at your favorite retail outlet.

COMING NEXT MONTH

It's a month of your favorite wedding themes! Don't miss:

#1234 AND BABY MAKES SIX—Pamela Dalton

Fabulous Fathers/It's A Girl!

Single father Devlin Hamilton agreed to a *platonic* marriage with lovely Abby O'Reilly. Their children needed a real family—and Devlin and Abby could help each other without the added risk of true love. Until a surprisingly passionate wedding night led to a new family addition!

#1235 THREE KIDS AND A COWBOY—Natalie Patrick

Second Chance At Marriage

Playing the part of the loving wife wasn't difficult for Miranda Sykes. She still loved her soon-to-be ex-husband, and Brodie needed her to adopt the orphans he'd taken in. But Miranda hadn't realized that three kids and a cowboy just might change her mind about staying around forever!

#1236 JUST SAY I DO—Lauryn Chandler

Substitute Groom

A fake engagement to dashing Adam Garrett would finally rid once-jilted bride Annabelle of everyone's pity. But when sparks started to fly between her and her substitute groom, their arrangement didn't feel like a game anymore! Could Annabelle get Adam to just say "I do" for real?

#1237 THE BEWILDERED WIFE—Vivian Leiber

The Bride Has Amnesia!

Dean Radcliffe's nanny had lost her memory…and thought she was Dean's wife and mother of his children! Until Susan remembered the truth, the handsome single father had to play along, but could it be this bewildered woman was meant to *truly* be his wife?

#1238 HAVE HONEYMOON, NEED HUSBAND—Robin Wells

Runaway Bride

After jilting her two-timing fiancé, Josie Randall decided to go on her dude ranch honeymoon—alone. Falling for wrangler Luke O'Dell was the last thing she'd expected—but the brooding, stubborn rancher soon lassoed her love, and had her hoping this honeymoon could land Luke as a husband!

#1239 A GROOM FOR MAGGIE—Elizabeth Harbison

Green Card Marriage

A marriage of convenience to her arrogant boss was drastic, but Maggie Weller would do anything to stay with Alex Harrison—and care for his adorable little girl. But Maggie's green-card wedding led not only to a permanent position in Alex's home, but to a most *unexpected* place in his heart!